Lock Down Publications and Ca$h Presents

LOVE ME OR LET ME GO 2

THE OTHER SIDE OF FOREVER

Written By

R. FACEY

First Edition 2026

Printed in the United States of America

Lock Down Publications
P.O. Box 944
Stockbridge, GA 30281
www.lockdownpublications.com

Like our page on Facebook: Lock Down Publications
www.facebook.com/lockdownpublications.ldp

Stay Connected with Us!

Text **LOCKDOWN** to 22828 to stay up-to-date with new releases, sneak peaks, contests and more…

Like our page on Facebook:
Lock Down Publications

Join Lock Down Publications/The New Era Reading Group

Visit our website:
www.lockdownpublications.com

Follow us on Instagram:
Lock Down Publications

Email Us: We want to hear from you!

Acknowledgements

Another one, thank you. To the Most High always, much gratitude is given. My honorable mentions for this one is Tyra, Snoop and Meme. Thank y'all. Sequoyah, Dolly, Azaria, the first ones to snatch them and read them. Cee, Lala, Sabrina, Ty, Disney, Asia, Lele. To my author sister, Nikki K. Hail that pushes me every day to write; to my friend, my Nashe'aaaaa. One of the most solid and genuine individuals I've met in this prison experience. To my brother Joe that rarely says no, thank you. To everyone that reposts, posts and supports my books, thank you. To the ones in chain gang with me, we on the way. To my rock always, Santana, I love your life. F R E E Y O U. To Cash, thank you for making this author journey easy, thank you for hearing me.

To my friend Tevin "T-Hood" Hood 7 whose name is used for the character of "Tool", I hope the life he exudes is a direct testament of the love you've shown in this world. Long Live The Z.

Prologue

Sacavè

I found out the way everybody found out about everything now.

Social media.

Wasn't even looking for it. I was just scrolling and then it just popped up.

A post. Reshared by somebody we both knew. Somebody who probably didn't even think about whether I would see it. Probably just hit repost without a second thought because why would they. It had been over a year. People moved on. That was just what happened.

Congratulations to the beautiful bride.

I stopped scrolling.

There she was.

Kia.

In a white dress that was everything that dress was supposed to be on a woman that looked like her.

She was happy.

I put my phone down.

Picked it back up.

Put it down again.

I wasn't gon' lie to myself and say I didn't see this coming. I had known Kia for long enough to know that she wasn't the type to stay still in her pain. She processed and she healed and she moved forward and she did all of it with a kind of intention that I had always admired even when it was directed away from me. She wasn't built to be broken permanently. I knew that.

I just hadn't expected it to look like this.

A whole wedding. A smile I hadn't seen on her face in longer than I wanted to admit even to myself.

I picked the phone back up and looked at the picture one more time.

She got married.

Kia is somebody's wife.

And the somebody wasn't me.

I had told myself for a long time that I was okay with how things ended. That I understood it. That I had made the choices that led to where we landed and I owned that and I was moving forward.

I believed that right up until I saw that picture.

Because seeing it didn't feel like moving forward. It felt like something was sitting in the middle of my chest.

I wasn't angry at her. I needed to be clear about that even inside my own head. She had every right. More than every right. What I had put her through, what I had allowed to happen, what I had been too locked in my own damage to prevent, she owed me nothing. Not her time. Not her forgiveness. Not a second thought.

She owed me nothing and she had given him everything.

And I was standing in my kitchen on a random Tuesday looking at evidence of that on a phone screen and feeling something I had no right to feel.

That was the honest truth of it.

I had no right.

Didn't stop it from feeling the way it felt.

I picked the phone back up one more time.

Looked at her face.

That smile.

Then I turned the screen off and put the phone in my pocket and went and found something else to do with my hands because standing still with that feeling wasn't something I was built for and the only thing worse than feeling it was letting it see me feeling it.

She was happy.

That was supposed to be enough.

I was gon’ make it enough.

Chapter 1

San Juan, PR

"Damn, it's hot out this muhfucka," Tool complained, stopping dead in his tracks to pull his hoodie off.

"It is," I said, fanning myself with my hand because I couldn't shed a single layer wearing this skintight *Lululemon* set.

This was my first time in Puerto Rico. First time on a plane in my adult life if we're being honest. And Tool had made the whole experience easy the way he made everything easy lately. First class flights where the seats reclined all the way back, a five-star hotel that looked like something out of a magazine, excursions already booked and paid for before we even landed. All I had to do was show up in all my fineness, and I had that part covered with no problem.

"We going straight to the hotel, dropping these bags, then hitting the beach. Keep it light though, we got dinner reservations at *1919* tonight," Tool said, scrolling through his phone while we waited on our Uber.

I looked at him with the biggest grin and just nodded, still not fully believing any of this was real.

"What?" he asked, catching my smile and giving it right back, then leaning over to kiss my forehead.

"Just happy to be here," I said softly. "With you."

"Me too, baby," he said, and kissed me properly that time.

The Uber pulled up bumping some reggaeton that perfectly fit the whole vibe of where we were. The driver hopped out with a big smile and opened our door. "Hop in. I load bags."

I got quiet on the ride over, just taking everything in. Colorful buildings painted in pinks and yellows and blues. Palm trees swaying. The ocean stretching out further than my eyes could follow. It was beautiful out here. Different from Atlanta. More vibrant. More alive.

Tool grabbed my hand. "You good?"

"Yeah," I said. "Just thinking about Saviour."

"Baby, he's just fine. We'll call him when we get to the hotel," he said, easy and unbothered.

We. That inclusive shit. The way he made me feel like I never had to carry nothing alone, like we were already a team before we even had the title, was so refreshing I didn't know what to do with it sometimes. I laid my head on his shoulder. "Thank you."

"You need this. We need this," he said. "When's the last time you did something just for you?"

I thought about it. Really thought about it. And I couldn't come up with a single answer. Everything I did was for Saviour, for my family, for friends, for Sacavè's ungrateful ass.

"Exactly," Tool said, reading my face the way he always did. "We 'bout to live it up for the next four days. A'ight?"

I squeezed his hand and nodded.

***

About fifteen minutes later, we pulled up to the hotel. Two beautiful women in matching uniforms were already outside holding trays of fresh fruit and frozen margaritas in fancy glasses.

"Welcome to the Condado Vanderbilt Hotel," they greeted with warm smiles.

"Thank you," I said, grabbing one of them margaritas before I even got both feet on the ground. Tool did the same and tipped them each a twenty without even breaking his stride.

This hotel was nice as hell. Not nice like the Marriott your auntie books for family reunions. Like *nigga got money* type nice and want you to know it the second you walk in. The marble floors were so clean I could see myself in them. Chandeliers that looked like they cost more than my mama's house. Fresh flowers on every surface like somebody's whole job was just keeping this place smelling good. Soft music was playing from somewhere I couldn't even see where. I didn't know what to do with myself. I just held onto Tool's arm and tried not to look too impressed.

I was already in my feelings and we hadn't even made it past the lobby.

Tool handled everything like he did this every day. Checked us in smooth, got the room keys and our all-inclusive wristbands, even spoke Spanish to the front desk lady and made her giggle. I did nothing but exist on his arm and, honestly, I loved every second of it.

The bellhop took our bags ahead of us while the concierge walked us through everything, the restaurants, the spa, the pool, the beach access. I was taking it all in, not just the hotel but the feeling. What it felt like to be taken care of. To be spoiled. To just *be* without having to manage or plan or hold everything together by myself.

The elevator opened on our floor, and Tool guided me down the hall with his hand at the small of my back. He slid the keycard in and pushed the door open.

One bed. One big, beautiful bed draped in crisp, white sheets that looked expensive enough to pay my rent. It was stacked with so many decorative pillows it looked like a fortress, a clean canvas waiting for us to mess it up.

We had sex for the first time just a couple days before this trip and it was good, real good, so whether we would be sharing that bed wasn't even a question.

"This cool?" Tool asked, watching me take it all in.

"This is *nice*," I said, walking straight toward the floor-to-ceiling windows.

The room was everything. Ocean view so blue and perfect it looked like a high-end painting, not something I was actually standing in front of. A balcony with two chairs and a table just waiting for a bottle of something cold. A plush sitting area that screamed luxury, and a bathroom bigger than my bedroom back home, complete with a deep soaking tub and a rain shower that probably cost more than my car. Tool had really went all out, no shortcuts, no budget, just pure unadulterated "you're with me now" energy.

"A'ight, I'm 'bout to hop in the shower real quick then we can head down to the beach," Tool said, already pulling his shirt over his head.

Lord have mercy.

I had seen him shirtless before but every single time felt like the first time. Broad shoulders that took up all the space in the room, a defined chest, and those abs . . . they looked carved out of something that wasn't even human. Just dark solid power.

"You drooling, baby," he said, smirking without even looking up.

"Shut up," I said, grabbing a pillow off the bed and throwing it at him.

He caught it with one hand, laughed, and disappeared into the bathroom. I heard the shower turn on a few seconds later.

I started unpacking both our bags while he was in there, hanging up my dresses and swimsuits, organizing his button-ups and linen pants, and lining our shoes up in the closet. I had packed for every possible scenario. Tamia had helped me, and she had made sure I wasn't out here slipping in a single outfit.

"Sista, you gotta take the sexy red swimsuit," she had said, folding it and sliding it into my suitcase with that knowing look she always had. "That's the *I-just-filed-for-divorce-and-I'm living-my-best-life* vibe."

I thought about Saviour and FaceTimed him before I could talk myself out of it. He answered on the second ring, Sacavè's living room in the background.

"Hey, big boy. You okay?" I asked.

"Yes, Mommy. I got a gold star, look." He held it up to the camera with the biggest smile on his face.

My mommy guilt knocked on the door immediately. I hated missing moments like this.

"Oh, wow, that's nice," I said, cheesing so hard my cheeks hurt. "What did you get it for?"

"For being a good listener. And Ms. Marie said I helped clean up the best," he said, bouncing in his seat like he couldn't contain himself.

"Wow, baby. I'm so proud of you. Mommy's big boy," I said.

"Mommy, did you get on the plane already?" he asked, his little face all curious.

"Yes, baby. It was so much fun. I can't wait to take you next time," I said.

His eyes went wide. "Really?"

"Really. I promise," I said.

"Okay. When are you coming back?" he asked.

"Four more days, okay?" I said, holding up four fingers.

He counted on his little fingers real serious. "One, two, three, four. Four more days, okay Mommy."

"That's right, baby. I love you so much," I said.

"I love you too. Bye, Mommy." He blew kisses at the screen and hung up.

I looked up just as Tool opened the bathroom door, steam pouring out around him. He was standing there in just a towel wrapped low around his waist, water still dripping down his chest and abs like he was posing on purpose. I had already changed into my swimsuit, a black two-piece.

"Damn," he said, stopping dead. "You trying to start something before we even leave this room?"

"Boy, I'm trying to see this beach," I said, knowing exactly what I was doing and enjoying every second of his reaction.

He unwrapped the towel and started drying off, completely unbothered by his own nakedness. And I mean his body was perfect, abs, arms, tight ass, and his dick just hanging there slightly curved to the left, already starting to wake up just from looking at me. He was getting me back and he knew it. He started fishing through his bag for something, moving slow on purpose, drawing the whole thing out.

"Lotion? Right here," I said, grabbing the cocoa butter off the nightstand. "I got you."

I started with his chest, rubbing slow circles, feeling his muscles tense under my hands. He looked down at me, licking his lips, and I felt the energy in that whole room shift. I moved to his arms next, biceps, elbows, wrists, taking my time like I had nowhere to be. Then I squatted down to do his thighs, and his dick jumped and stiffened right in front of my face like it was introducing itself.

I gave it soft little pecks while I kept rubbing the lotion into his thighs, acting like I didn't notice it getting harder with every kiss.

"Sit down so I can get your feet," I said all sweet and innocent.

I felt his eyes on me, dark, heavy, and hungry, tracking every single movement as I worked. I didn't just rub his feet; I worshipped them, my thumbs digging deep between his toes with a slow, agonizing precision that had him tensing under my touch. I massaged his ankles, and let my hands glide up his calves slowly, my palms slick with cocoa butter, moving with a rhythm that was steady and sensual.

"Ouu," he moaned, his head dropping back, exposing the hard line of his throat.

I stood up, the movement fluid and cat-like. I took my time rubbing the leftover lotion into my elbows, my eyes never leaving his, making him wait for the next move. I was in total control, and the air between us was so thick it felt like it could combust.

"Lay back," I said, pulling my braids up into a bun.

He listened, his body sinking into the mattress, his chest heaving as he tried to catch a breath that was already gone.

I took my time with him, slow at first, then with more intention, working him until his breathing changed and his grip on the back of my head tightened. He was trying to warn me, but I wasn't going nowhere. I wanted all of it.

He released, and I swallowed every bit of it. Then he pulled me up by my face and kissed me deep and slow, like I had just done something that deserved to be honored. He reached for the strings on my swimsuit bottoms, and I stopped his hands.

"No," I said, standing up and fixing my top. "It pleased me to please you. Now let's go see this beach."

I used his own line right back on him, the same one he had hit me with when he had gone down on me and wouldn't let me reciprocate. Tool laughed, shaking his head slow. "A'ight. But don't blame me for later."

"Don't threaten me with a good time," I said, smirking.

He got dressed in white linen shorts and a fitted tank that showed off every muscle in both arms while I packed our beach bag with sunscreen, towels, and room keys. Then we headed out, his hand at my lower back the whole way down the hall.

***

The beach was everything. White sand so soft it felt like powder between my toes. Water so clear and blue it looked fake, like somebody had photoshopped it into the background of real life. A breeze just strong enough to keep the heat from being too much. Our room came with its own little palm-covered canopy and two beach chairs already set up and waiting. I dropped my cover-up the second we got there and ran straight to the water without waiting for anybody.

"Come on," I yelled back at Tool, who had settled into one of the chairs with his arms behind his head, watching me like he had all the time in the world. I put my hand on my hip and waited. He got up slow on purpose, taking his sweet time, laughing the whole way over.

"I'm coming, I'm coming. Damn, woman," he said, jogging the last few steps.

The water was perfect, warm but refreshing, the kind that made you want to stay in it until your fingers pruned. I waded in until it was waist-deep, and Tool came up behind me. I wrapped my legs around his waist while he held me up like it was nothing.

"This is perfect," I said.

We stayed in that water for hours, playing around like we were kids, splashing, floating on our backs, just *being*. At one point Tool tried to dunk me and I screamed loud enough that people on the beach started looking over and laughing with us. I didn't even care. That's how good it felt to just exist somewhere with no noise, no Saviour schedule, no nothing, just him and me and that water. When we finally got out, we laid on our towels side by side and let the sun dry us off and warm our skin back up.

"Thank you for this," I said, turning on my side to look at him.

"For what?"

"For all of it. For being patient with me. For waiting for me to get my shit together," I said.

He tilted my chin up so I had to look him in the eyes. "Kia, stop thanking me for doing what I'm supposed to do. A nigga's supposed to pursue what he wants, be patient with what's worth it, and be delicate with what's valuable." He looked at me steady. "You're all three."

He started pressing soft kisses to my lips, each one saying what words couldn't cover. "So thank you for being sunshine. For being worth all this."

I blinked back the tears that tried to come, smiling instead. We stayed like that until the sky started doing that thing it did right before sunset, turning orange and pink and purple all at once.

"We should head back and get ready for dinner," Tool said, standing and pulling me up with him.

***

Back in the room, we showered together. I washed his back, tracing the tattoo across his shoulder blades with my soapy hands. He washed mine, running his palms down my spine slowly, stopping at the Chinese characters tattooed there.

"What this mean?" he asked, his fingers tracing each one.

"Devotion to family," I said.

"That's beautiful, baby," he said, and kissed the back of my neck.

After the shower, I got dressed while Tool sat on the bed scrolling his phone. I wore my yellow sundress, one that made my skin glow and showed off my shape without screaming for attention. I laid my baby hairs, pulled my braids into a half-up, half-down style, and kept my makeup simple but pretty.

I loved how Tool brought this side of me out, the side that wanted to put in the extra effort, that wanted to feel pretty just because, that had been tucked away somewhere between becoming a mama and surviving a marriage that was never really whole. It felt good to let her back out.

When I came out of the bathroom, Tool was sitting on the edge of the bed, already dressed in his linen button-up and slacks. The way he looked at me when I walked out made my whole body warm up.

"Damn, baby. You look good," he said, standing to turn me around slow and get the full picture.

"You too," I said, walking over to fix his collar even though it didn't need fixing. I just wanted a reason to put my hands on him.

"Ready?" he asked, offering me his arm.

I grabbed my clutch and took it.

***

The restaurant was intimate in the best way. Dim lighting, candles on every table, and the ocean visible through the floor-to-ceiling windows like it was part of the decor.

"Good evening. My name is Samia. Can I start you with something to drink?" our server asked, her accent thick and beautiful.

"Passion fruit mojito," I said.

"Make that two," Tool added.

When she walked off, he reached across the table and took my hand. "Real shit, how you feeling?"

I took a breath and actually sat with the question before I answered it. "Free," I said. "I feel free."

"That's what I want for you," he said, rubbing his thumb across my knuckles. "Always."

"You make me happy," I said softly.

"We make each other happy," he corrected, squeezing my hand.

Our drinks came. We ordered; I got the mofongo with shrimp, he got the churrasco steak. The food was everything, especially when I started stealing bites off his plate and mixing it with mine. We talked through all of dinner, laughed through most of it, and I don't think either one of us wanted it to end. After, we walked the beach one more time, shoes in our hands, feet in the sand, waves crashing nearby, the whole sky above us doing too much.

"I could stay here forever," I said.

"We can come back whenever you want. This just the first of many," he said.

"Many, huh? You must know I'll be around?" I teased.

"For life," he said, and stopped walking to look at me like he meant every syllable of it. "I know we ain't been together that long. But I know what I want. And what I want is you. For as long as you'll have me."

"I want that too," I whispered.

He kissed me right there under that moonlight with the waves coming in and the warm breeze moving, and I swear if I could've frozen one moment in time, it would've been that one right there.

***

Back in the room, Tool closed the door behind us and before I could even take off my heels, he had me pressed against the wall, kissing me like he had been holding back all night, which he had. I had felt it in the way his hand made slow circles on my thigh the whole Uber ride back.

He picked me up, my legs finding his waist naturally, and carried me to the bed. Heels came off first. Then my dress. His shirt. His pants. Until it was just us and nothing between us and the kind of quiet that only existed when everything felt exactly right.

"You're so beautiful, Kia," he had said, his eyes moving over me slow like he was memorizing something.

I felt exposed in the best way. Vulnerable but safe. And that right there was how I knew this was different from anything I had known before. He kissed down my neck, across my collarbone, taking his time with every part of me on the way down until he was between my thighs and I couldn't think straight enough to form a complete sentence.

"Tool," I breathed.

"I got you, baby," he said.

And he did.

When he finally slid inside me, I swear everything went quiet. The stretch, the fullness, the way our bodies just fit together like we had been doing this for years and not days.

"Fuck, baby," he groaned. "You feel so good."

"Don't stop," I said, my nails finding his back.

We moved together, his whispered words in my ear, my nails in his skin, both of us chasing something that kept getting better the closer we got to it. When I came, it washed over me in a wave that shook my whole body. He came right after, groaning into my neck, holding me tight while everything in him let go. We laid there after in the quiet, both of us breathing hard, both of us gone.

"That was—" I started.

"I know," he said, pulling me into him before I could finish. He kissed my forehead and pulled the covers over us.

"We got four more days," he said.

"I don't know if I'm gonna survive," I said.

"You will," he said. "I'm gonna make sure of it."

I fell asleep in his arms, feeling safer and more loved than I had in longer than I could remember.

Chapter 2

Sacavè

While Kia was in Puerto Rico living it up with that nigga, I'm sitting in my living room at 2 AM on a Tuesday with a bottle of Hennessy, trying not to crash the fuck out.

Saviour is upstairs asleep. I had him since she left. Him being around was the only thing keeping me from completely losing my shit.

I couldn't sleep. Hadn't slept right in days, not the kind of sleep that actually rests you. I just laid in bed staring at the ceiling until the shadows started playing tricks on my eyes. My mind was a war zone, racing with thoughts I couldn't shut off, memories of her looping like a car crash I couldn't look away from. Every time I closed my eyes, I saw her with him. Finally, I gave up, the silence getting too loud to be handled, and went downstairs to let the Hennessy calm my nerves some more.

The bottle was already half empty. I had been at it since midnight, sitting here in the dark with just the glow from the TV I wasn't even watching. I fucked around and ended up on Facebook, scrolling through my timeline when I saw picture after picture of her ass in Puerto Rico looking happy as hell.

Meanwhile, she still got my last name. I locked my phone and took another drink, the liquor burning going down but not enough to numb what I was feeling.

My phone buzzed with a text from Sena: *I can't sleep. I know you probably can't either. Please just talk to me.*

I stared at the message. This bitch had been hitting me up non-stop for days, and I had been ignoring every single one.

My mind went back to three days ago. To when I found out what she did.

***

Three Days Earlier…

It was Sunday afternoon. Me and Saviour had just got back from Dave & Buster's where I had let him run wild on the games, winning enough tickets to get some cheap-ass toy he would probably forget about by tomorrow.

"Daddy, I'm hungry!" Saviour said, running into the living room.

"A'ight, man. Go wash your hands. I'll make you a sandwich," I said.

While he was in the bathroom, I sat down on the couch and pulled out my phone to check my emails. I had been avoiding them all weekend, not wanting to deal with work shit on my time with my son. That's when I saw it, an email dated two days prior with the subject line:

Subject: **Sanders v. Sanders - Divorce Proceedings Update**

I opened that shit, scanning through all that legal talk until I got to the part that said:

"We have received the signed divorce petition from the petitioner's counsel. Your signature has been verified, and we are proceeding with scheduling the final hearing. Please contact our office at your earliest convenience."

What the fuck?

Your signature has been verified. But I never signed shit. I had them papers in my old whip, in the driver's side door, where I put them the day Kia handed them to me months ago.

I jumped up and went straight to the garage where my M6 had been sitting since I bought the Durango. Opened the driver's door and checked that door pocket.

Empty.

I tore through the whole car, the glove box, center console, under the seats, in the trunk, everywhere. Nothing. Them papers were gone. I stood there in the garage, confused.

"Daddy, I'm ready," Saviour yelled from inside the house.

I took a deep breath, trying to calm myself down. I couldn't let my son see me like this, couldn't let him know something was wrong.

"Hold on, son," I called back, closing the car door.

I made Saviour his sandwich, peanut butter and jelly, cut diagonal the way he liked, and sat with him at the table while he ate and told me about all the games he had played.

"And then I got the jackpot on the spinning thing, Daddy. Did you see?" he said, his mouth full.

"I saw, man. That was dope," I said, but my mind was elsewhere.

An hour later, Kia pulled up to get Saviour.

"Hey, baby," she said to Saviour when she walked in, bending down to hug him.

"Hi, Mommy. Look what I got," he said, showing her the cheap plastic dinosaur he had picked out.

"That's so cool. Go get your stuff, okay? Mommy's gonna talk to Daddy for a minute," she said.

Saviour ran upstairs, and Kia turned to me, her smile fading when she saw my face.

"What's wrong?" she asked.

"Did you sign my name on them divorce papers?" I asked straight up.

Her face went from confused to shocked. "What?"

"Because my attorney just sent me an email saying my signature was verified and they moving forward with the hearing. But I never signed shit, Kia," I said, watching her face closely for any sign she was lying.

"Sacavè, I swear to God I didn't sign your name. I filed my petition, yeah, but I didn't forge nothing," she said.

I believed her. The look on her face, the way her voice went up, she was telling the truth.

"Then who the fuck did?" I asked, more to myself than to her.

"I don't know, but it wasn't me," she said firmly.

Saviour came running back downstairs with his backpack and iPad, breaking the tension.

"Ready, Mommy," he said.

"Okay, baby. Say bye to Daddy," Kia said, her eyes still on me with concern.

"Bye, Daddy. Love you," Saviour said, hugging my leg.

"Love you too, man. See you in a few days," I said, bending down to kiss his forehead.

After they left, I stood in my living room, my mind racing. As soon as the thought crossed my mind, I knew. Sena was gonna pull up any minute. She usually did on Sundays after my weekends with Saviour because I made her leave when I had my son so I could spend quality time with him.

Sena was the only other person besides me and Kia with access to my cars. She had been at my crib on and off for months. She knew where everything was. She had keys to my house, knew my routines, had access to all my shit.

I pulled out my phone and called her. No answer. Called again. Straight to voicemail.

"Yo, you need to call me back. Right the fuck now," I said after the beep.

I went back inside, pacing back and forth in the living room like a caged animal. My mind was going crazy. *Did she really do this shit? Would she really forge my signature on legal documents?* That's some criminal-ass shit.

Twenty minutes later, I heard keys jingling in the door. She walked in all smiles, holding two Chipotle bags like everything was normal.

"Hey. I got us food. I got you that steak bowl you like with—" she started.

"Where them papers at?" I cut her off, my voice low and dangerous.

Her smile dropped quick. "What papers?"

"Don't fuck with me right now, Sena. The divorce papers. The ones that were in my car. Where the fuck they at?" I said, my voice getting louder with each word.

She set the bags down on the counter slowly, and I watched her whole face change. She looked confused, concerned even, like she was really trying to help.

"When was the last time you seen them?" she asked, walking toward the garage like she was about to help me search.

I let her play her little game for about ten minutes. Watching her pretend to look. Watching her act like she gave a fuck. Watching her help me search for papers she knew damn well she had already taken and signed. I even said, "Man, this divorce shit about to make me lose my son," just to see if she would crack, if she would show any remorse.

She didn't even budge. Just kept searching, kept up the act.

Finally, I couldn't take it no more. I walked back in the house, and she followed me, still playing her role.

"So you telling me you don't know shit about my signature magically appearing on papers I never fuckin' signed?" I asked.

She looked away, and that's when I knew for sure.

"Sena, look at me," I said, my voice calm but deadly. "Did you sign my name on them papers?"

Silence.

"*Sena,*" I yelled, and she jumped, tears already in her eyes.

"I did," she finally screamed back, her voice breaking. "I did it."

"That wasn't your fuckin' call to make," I yelled, my whole body shaking with rage.

"She wanted it. The relationship was over anyway," Sena cried, reaching for me.

I stepped back like she had a disease. "Nah. Nah, fuck that. You don't get to make that decision for me."

"The relationship was over. She didn't want you anymore," she insisted, tears streaming down her face.

"Let me make that choice my damn self," I yelled.

"She was never gon' make you happy," Sena shot back.

"And you think you would? You think after this foul-ass shit you pulled, I could ever trust yo' sneaky ass again?" I asked, my voice dripping with disgust.

The look on her face almost made me feel bad. Almost. But then I remembered what she did, how she violated my trust in the worst possible way, and any sympathy I had disappeared.

Then I just started throwing everything she owned out of my house. Wigs off the bathroom counter. Bonnets from my dresser. Body sprays from the nightstand. Phone chargers. Clothes from the closet. Shoes by the door. Everything.

"Get all your shit out my spot, Sena," I yelled, opening my front door and tossing her stuff onto the porch.

"Sacavè, please, I was trying to help you," she sobbed.

"Get your muhfuckin' shit and get out," I repeated, louder this time, my voice echoing through the house.

She stood there crying, waiting for me to take it back, to calm down, to forgive her. She stuffed everything into two big-ass duffel bags, crying the whole time.

"I'm sorry," she whispered as she headed to the door, her bags barely zipped. "I really am. I thought I was helping you."

"Foul-ass shit," I said, my back to her, unable to even look at her anymore.

I heard the door close, then her car start, then the sound of her driving away. And that was it. My best friend since we were kids. Gone.

***

I had been drinking ever since that day. The way Kia flew her ass out of town with another nigga just days later showed me how she really felt. She didn't give a fuck about me, about us, about the ten-plus years we had spent together.

I tried to talk to her about it multiple times, called her, texted her, even pulled up to her house once. But she didn't care. It was a done deal in her eyes. She was done with me, and nothing was gonna change that.

She told me how Sena had put the papers on her truck on the day she got her promotion, left them there with a congratulations balloon like it was some kind of joke. Then she said it was kinda hard to believe I didn't sign the papers myself because I had started acting distant toward her around that same time.

And she was right. I had been distant. But that was only because Sena had been in my ear about them panties she had found, about me fucking Kia again, about how I was playing myself trying to hold on to someone who didn't want me.

I told Kia I had even picked up overtime at work just to get away from all of it, to not have to think about the divorce or Sena or any of that shit. She pretended to understand why I was acting like that, nodded along like she got it. But she still wanted the divorce. Nothing I said changed her mind.

I looked at Sena's text again on my phone screen. A part of me wanted to respond, but I wasn't ready to forgive her. Wasn't ready to let her back in. I would probably never be ready. What she did crossed a line that couldn't be uncrossed.

I didn't respond. Just took another drink and turned on the TV. Some old *Martin* reruns were playing, the episode where Martin lost his Varnell Hill CD and had Gina backed into a corner like she robbed a bank, interrogating everybody in the house over a fifteen-dollar piece of plastic that was in his own shit the whole time. That episode used to have me and Kia crying laughing. Now I couldn't even crack a smile.

It just reminded me of what I had lost.

Between Kia being in Puerto Rico living her best life and Sena forging my signature like I was too stupid to make my own decisions, I felt like the two people I had trusted most in this world had played me. And sitting here at 2 AM drinking Hennessy straight from the bottle was the only way I knew how to deal with that shit.

Hours passed. The *Martin* reruns turned into *Fresh Prince*, then some infomercial I wasn't paying attention to. I dozed off on the couch until my alarm went off at 6 AM, waking me up.

Time to get Saviour up and ready for school.

I got up, my head pounding, my mouth dry as hell. I put the Hennessy bottle back in the freezer and went to the half-bathroom downstairs. Splashed cold water on my face, looked at myself in the mirror. I looked like shit. Eyes bloodshot, face ashy, beard uneven.

I went upstairs and opened Saviour's door quietly. He was still knocked out, curled up with his toy elephant, his little chest rising and falling peacefully.

"Savy, wake up, man. Time for school," I said, sitting on the edge of his bed.

"Nooo," he mumbled, pulling the covers over his head, his voice muffled.

"Come on, son. You gotta get up," I said, shaking him gently, rubbing his back.

He finally opened his eyes and looked at me, squinting.

"Morning, Daddy," he said, yawning.

"Morning, lil' man. Let's get you ready," I said, helping him out of bed, his little body still warm from sleep.

***

The morning routine was rough as hell. My head was killing me, pounding with every movement, and I was moving slow as hell. Saviour wasn't much of a morning person either, he got that from me, but I managed to get him fed, dressed, teeth brushed, and in the car by 7:45.

I gotta give Kia her props for doing this shit five days out of the week by herself. This morning routine was no joke, especially with a hangover.

"Daddy, can we listen to my music?" Saviour asked from the backseat as I backed out the driveway.

"Yeah, man," I said, connecting his playlist through Bluetooth. Some kid-friendly rap shit that he liked, Kidz Bop versions of songs.

I dropped him off at school at 8:05, walked him to the door like I always did, watched him run inside and wave at me through the glass. Then I sat in the parking lot for a minute with my head against the steering wheel, trying to gather the energy to face the day.

My phone rang. Work. My supervisor's name flashed on the screen.

I ignored it.

It rang again. Same person.

I ignored that too, sending it to voicemail. I should've gone to work. I knew I should've. So I went back home and slept some more, collapsing on my bed fully clothed, not even bothering to take off my shoes.

***

When I woke up, it was past 1 PM. My phone had six missed calls. Three from work, two from my mama, one from my sister Faith.

I called my mama back first. If Faith was calling, she either wanted money or a ride to work, and I wasn't in the mood for neither.

"Where you been? I been calling you all morning," Ma said as soon as she answered.

"I'm at the crib," I said, my voice still hoarse from sleep and liquor.

"You sound terrible. You sick?" she asked.

"Nah, I'm straight. Just tired," I lied, rubbing my face.

"Mmhmm. I'm coming over after I get off work. We need to talk," she said in that tone that meant she wasn't asking.

"Ma, I'm good—"

"I'll be there at 5:00. Make sure you there," she said and hung up before I could argue.

Fuck.

***

I spent the rest of the afternoon trying to pull myself together. Took a long shower, letting the hot water beat down on my back. Brushed my teeth twice to get rid of the liquor taste. Put on clean clothes, a fresh white tee and some joggers. Tried to make the house look like I had my shit together, wiping down counters, straightening up the living room.

After all that, I realized I needed to turn around and pick Saviour back up by 3:15. I left early, got there at 3:00, and sat in the pickup line scrolling through my phone, trying to kill time. More texts from Sena. Five new ones since this morning. I didn't even read them. Just deleted the notifications without opening them.

Thirty minutes later, Saviour came running out the building, his backpack bouncing on his shoulders. When he saw my truck, his whole face lit up like Christmas morning. Shit never got old.

"Daddy," he yelled, running over as fast as his little legs could carry him.

I got out to meet him halfway, scooping him up. "What's good, lil' man? School was straight?"

"Yes. We had art today and I made you a picture," he said excitedly, already digging in his backpack.

He pulled out a drawing, me, him, and Kia holding hands under a sun. *Happy Family* written across the top in his messy handwriting. A family that didn't exist no more. Looking at that shit did something to me.

"That's nice, son. We putting that on the fridge when we get home," I said, trying to keep it together for him.

"Can we get Chick-fil-A?" he asked, looking up at me with those big eyes.

"Yeah, we can do that," I said, buckling him into his car seat.

***

We hit the drive-through, got his usual 4-count nuggets with waffle fries and a lemonade. By the time we got home, it was almost 4:30. Saviour ran inside and went straight to the living room with his food, ready to turn on cartoons.

"Eat at the table, Savy," I said, catching him before he could settle in.

"But Daddy—"

"Table. Now," I said, not having the energy to argue or explain.

He grabbed his food and moved to the kitchen table, pouting the whole time, his bottom lip stuck out. I sat across from him with my own food, a Spicy Chicken Sandwich I had no appetite for. My stomach was still fucked up from all the drinking.

"Daddy, not hungry?" Saviour asked, looking up at me while dipping a nugget in Chick-fil-A sauce.

"Not really, man," I said, forcing myself to take a bite. I knew I had to tighten up if my five-year-old son could peep that something was wrong.

He nodded and went back to eating his nuggets, bobbing his head back and forth to some song in his head. My phone dinged. Text from my mama: *I'm on my way.*

***

Like clockwork, fifteen minutes later, there was a knock at the door. My mama. I let her in and she stopped in the doorway, looking me up and down. A full-blown standoff.

"You look like shit," she said bluntly, walking past me into the house.

"Good to see you too, Ma," I said, closing the door.

"*Sugaaaa*," Saviour yelled, abandoning his last nugget to run and hug her.

"Hey, my baby. How was school?" she asked, scooping him up even though he was getting too big for that, her face transforming into pure joy when she looked at him.

"Good. I made Daddy a picture," he said proudly.

"Let me see," she said, setting him down.

Saviour ran to get the drawing from where I had put it on the fridge and brought it back to show her. "That's so good, baby. You're such a good artist," she said, studying it carefully. Her face switched for a second when she saw what it was, the three of us as a happy family, but she didn't say nothing in front of him.

"Saviour, go upstairs and play for a minute. I need to talk to your daddy," she said, her voice still sweet for him.

"Okay," he said, running upstairs, his feet thundering on the steps.

As soon as he was gone, Ma turned to me, and her whole demeanor changed. "Sit down."

I sat on the couch. She sat across from me in the chair, her purse still on her shoulder.

"You called out of work again today, didn't you?" she asked, her eyes boring into me.

"How you know that?" I asked, even though I already knew the answer.

"Because your supervisor called me looking for you. At your big age, you still have me listed as your emergency contact," she said, shaking her head. "He said you been missing shifts all week. Said if you don't show up tomorrow, you're fired and it's out of his hands."

"Fuck," I muttered.

"Don't cuss me," she said sharply. "Now what's going on with you? And don't tell me nothing, because I can see it all over your face."

"Nothing, Ma. I'm handling it—"

"You're not handling nothing. Looks like it's handling you," she said, leaning forward. "Your sister showed me them pictures on Facebook. Kia in Puerto Rico with some new man, living her best life while you sitting here drinking yourself stupid."

I didn't say nothing.

"I know you," she continued. "I know you drinking. I can see it in your eyes, in your face. I can smell it on you even though you tried to cover it up with a shower."

"It ain't just that," I finally said. "Sena . . . she forged my signature on them divorce papers."

Ma's whole face changed, her expression going from concerned to shocked. "She did what?"

"Yeah. Found out a few days ago. So I lost my wife and my best friend in the same week," I said.

She was quiet for a minute. Then she got up and sat next to me on the couch, putting her arm around my shoulders.

"Baby, I'm sorry. I know that had to hurt," she said gently. "Sena been in your life since y'all was kids. Since elementary school. That's a deep betrayal."

"I know," I said.

"But you still gotta keep going," she said firmly. "You take it one day at a time. You go back to work tomorrow. You take care of your son. You eat right. You stop drinking. And eventually, it'll hurt less. But you gotta start somewhere. You gotta take that first step."

We sat there for a minute in silence, her arm around me, me trying not to break down completely.

"You hearing me?" she asked.

"I hear you, Ma," I said.

"Good. Now I'm going to Publix to get stuff for dinner. When I get back, we gon' eat like a family. Then you gon' put Saviour to bed, get some real sleep, and tomorrow you going back to work. You understand?" she said, standing up and grabbing her purse.

"Yes, ma'am," I said.

She kissed my forehead. "I love you, baby. But you gotta do better. For yourself and for that boy upstairs."

***

That night, after Ma cooked chicken pot pie, my favorite and left with hugs and reminders to "get yourself together;" after I put Saviour to bed and read him *The Very Hungry Caterpillar*, I laid in my own bed in the dark, staring at the ceiling.

No bottle. No music. Nothing to hide behind.

Chapter 3

Kia

The five days in Puerto Rico felt like a dream, but coming home felt even better. Not because I didn't love every second of that trip, but because I realized I was bringing that happiness back with me.

Tool drove us back from the airport, his hand on my thigh the whole ride while I dozed in and out of sleep in the passenger seat. Something about the way he drove made me feel safe. Like I could actually rest. When he pulled up to my house, I didn't want to get out. Didn't want the bubble we had been in for the past five days to pop.

"You good, baby?" he asked, rubbing my leg.

"Yeah, I'm good. Just tired. And I don't wanna leave you yet," I admitted.

"I know. But you gotta go get Saviour. He probably been driving his daddy crazy asking when you coming home," Tool said with a smile.

He was right. I had talked to Saviour every day while we were gone, and every single time he asked when I was coming back. Like he needed confirmation I hadn't forgotten about him. That always sat with me.

Tool got out and grabbed my suitcase from the back, then walked me inside. He set it down by the stairs and turned to me, pulling me in without a word.

"Call me when you get settled in with him. I wanna hear your voice before I go to sleep," he said into my hair.

"Okay," I said, not wanting to let go.

He kissed me, slow and deep, like he wasn't in a rush to be anywhere but right there. When he pulled back, he was smiling.

"Go get your baby. I'll talk to you later."

I watched him walk back to his truck, climb in, and pull off. Even after the best five days of my life, I was already missing him.

***

I took a quick shower to wash off the airport, then got back in my truck to head to Sacavè's. It was almost 8 PM, Saviour's bedtime, but knowing those two, Saviour had probably negotiated at least another hour out of him. That boy could talk his daddy into anything.

When I pulled up, before I could even reach for my phone, the front door swung open.

"Mommyyyy."

Saviour came flying down those steps in his pajamas, arms wide open, running so hard his little feet barely touched the ground. He hit me so fast I stumbled back a step, laughing, squeezing him so tight he squealed.

"Hey, baby. I missed you so much."

"I missed you too, Mommy. Daddy said you was getting me a surprise," he said into my neck.

I laughed. "Oh, he did, huh?"

"Mm-hmm."

I looked up and Sacavè was leaning in the doorway. He wasn't rushing out. Wasn't making a show of anything. He was just . . . still. Arms folded, watching us like he was taking a picture in his head he didn't want to forget. Something about the quiet in his face was harder to deal with than his attitude would've been.

I set Saviour down and walked up the steps. "Thanks for keeping him."

"That's my son. I don't watch him," Sacavè said.

Here we go.

"Saviour, go get your backpack and your iPad," I said.

"Okay." He disappeared inside, his little feet thundering down the hall.

Sacavè stepped back to give me room on the porch, but not far. He was quiet for a moment, looking out toward the street before he finally said, "You looked happy."

I blinked. "I was."

"Good," he said, and the word came out like it cost him something.

I didn't know what to do with that, so I didn't do anything.

"You really fuck with this nigga?" Sacavè asked, still not looking at me.

"His name is Tool. And I'm not doing this tonight," I said.

"I'm not doing nothing. I'm just asking." He finally looked at me then. "I'm Saviour's father. That mean something."

"Nobody said it didn't."

"Then act like it," he said. "I don't want him around my son, Kia."

I folded my arms. "You had Sena around our son for how long before we even separated? Don't come at me with that."

"That's different—"

"How? Explain it to me, Sacavè. How is it different?"

"Because Sena was already family. She was already in his life," he said.

"And now Tool is in mine. That means he's going to be in Saviour's life too. And from what I've seen? He's good with him." I paused, meeting his gaze. "Unless you got a real, actual reason, not jealousy, not ego, a real reason, then I don't know what you want me to say."

He was quiet. I could see him working through something, some argument he had rehearsed that wasn't landing the way he wanted it to.

"I just don't want Saviour getting attached to somebody who might not stick around," he finally said.

"He's going to be around," I said.

"You don't know that."

"I know him. And I know what he's shown me." I met his eyes. "That's more than I could say about a lot of things."

He looked away first. "A'ight." A pause. "Just make sure that nigga know Saviour got a daddy."

Then he walked back inside and the door closed behind him. I stood there for a second, letting that settle. It wasn't a threat. It wasn't even really an argument.

***

"Savy, did you have fun with Daddy?" I asked as we rode home. His little voice filled the back seat with stories about some cartoon they watched and the pancakes Sacavè made Saturday morning.

Within five minutes, mid-sentence, he was out. I glanced in the rearview mirror at him, head tilted, mouth barely open.

When we got home, I got him straight into bed. No bath, no arguments, no negotiations. Just tucked him in, pressed my lips to his forehead, and let him sleep. My phone buzzed on the nightstand.

Tool: *You get him?*

Me: *Yeah. He's already knocked out. About to get myself together and call you.*

Tool: *Take your time, baby. I know you tired.*

***

After I showered and got into my own bed, I laid there for a minute just feeling it. How good it felt to be home. How strange it was to be in my bed alone after five nights wrapped up in somebody who made that feel like the most natural thing in the world.

I grabbed my phone and FaceTimed him. He answered on the first ring, shirtless, in his bed, lamp on low behind him. Fine as sin and completely unbothered about it.

"There's my beautiful girl," he said, smiling like I had just made his night by calling.

"Hey, baby." I propped my phone on the nightstand and stretched out on my side.

"How's Saviour?"

"Knocked out. He was running on fumes." I smiled.

Tool laughed.

"He's a mess," I said, grinning.

"How was the pickup?" he asked, reading me the way he had been doing since the beginning.

I sighed. "He said he doesn't want you around Saviour."

Tool was quiet for a beat. His expression didn't go hard exactly, but it went still. Focused. "What you tell him?"

"I told him you weren't going anywhere."

He nodded slowly, holding my gaze through the phone. "Good. Because I meant what I said in Puerto Rico, Kia. Every word."

"I know," I said. "And I meant what I said back."

That landed between us, soft and sure, the way the truth does when there's nothing else competing with it. We talked for almost an hour about nothing, about everything, about the trip. Somewhere in the middle of it all, I forgot I was tired.

"So when am I seeing you again?" he asked.

"You just saw me," I laughed.

"I know. I'm greedy." He shrugged like he wasn't even sorry about it.

"This weekend. Saviour goes back to his dad Friday. We can do whatever," I said.

"Bet. I'm taking you somewhere nice."

"Where?"

"Surprise," he said with that smirk.

"Tool—"

"Goodnight, beautiful. Sweet dreams."

I rolled my eyes, but I was smiling so hard my face hurt. "Goodnight, baby."

Chapter 4

"Looking good, Kia," Jamila said as I passed her desk.

"Thank you, girl," I said, not breaking my stride.

It had been like that all morning. Compliments from everybody, double-takes in the hallway, Myra doing a full spin around me the second I walked through the door like I was a mannequin at the mall. I didn't know if it was because I had been working remote so much they had forgotten what I looked like, or if I was just radiating something different. Probably both. Happiness looks good on people. I had seen it on other women, and now I was wearing it myself.

I was filling out my clothes differently too. Tool had me out here eating good, restaurants two, three times a week, and he cooked on the nights we stayed in. Real food. Not *DoorDash*, not whatever I could throw together between Saviour's bath and bedtime. Actual meals. I had put on maybe seven, eight pounds, and every single one of them had landed exactly right.

Myra, of course, swore I was pregnant.

"I'm not," I told her flat out.

"You glowing though—"

"That's called being happy and eating real food, Myra. Me and that man use protection every single time. No babies outside of marriage." I paused. "Not that I'm even close to being anybody's wife right now. I still got about five more months being a Sanders."

She gave me a look. I gave her one back. That was the end of that conversation.

In-office days dragged. They always did now. Remote work had ruined me. I had gotten used to working in peace, on my own time, without the fluorescent lights and the background noise of people who had nothing better to do than walk past your desk three times in an hour. Today had the added joy of me having to train the new girl. She was taking my old position since I had moved up, which meant I had to sit with her for most of the afternoon and walk her through everything I used to do in my sleep.

She was pretty. I clocked that the second they brought her over to introduce her, mocha complexion, slim, natural hair pulled back neat. Professional. Quiet. She asked good questions and actually wrote things down, which I appreciated. I had no issues with her.

Until I noticed Trey.

He came over twice. *Twice.* The first time was almost believable, something about a system access form she needed to fill out. The second time he just happened to be walking by real slow, doing that thing men do when they're trying to look like they're not looking. I watched him clock her from across the room while she was still going through her onboarding modules: that familiar lean-in, that manufactured reason to exist in her vicinity.

I almost felt sorry for her.

Then I remembered I hadn't thought about Trey's little situation in months. Not since Tool had been taking very good care of everything that used to make me entertain less than what I deserved. Our sex life was a ten out of ten and somehow kept getting better every time, which I didn't think was physically possible, but here we were. And it came with all the other stuff too. Dates. Flowers for no reason. Trips. We had Destin coming up in three weeks, and I was already thinking about what I was going to pack.

He said he wanted to make it memorable.

I just hoped *memorable* didn't mean what I thought it might mean. Tool had been dropping little hints, *last name this, last name that*, and look, I don't have commitment issues. I was not afraid of love or of being somebody's person. I just wanted to stay right here for a little while longer. In this part. The part where everything was new and exciting and he was still finding new ways to surprise me. I needed to figure out who I was outside of being somebody's wife first. Sacavè had gotten a version of me that didn't fully know herself yet, and I wasn't about to repeat that.

Besides, his little comments about the divorce had dried up. He had obviously fell in line once the process moved forward, signature or not, cooperating or not, things were in motion and he knew it.

***

I was packing up at the end of the day when Myra materialized at my desk like she had been waiting for the office to thin out.

"So," she said, sitting on the edge of my desk without being invited. "You know who the new girl is?"

I glanced up. "Deja? I just trained her today."

"Trey lil' girlfriend."

I stopped. Looked at her. "Huh?"

"Trey got her hired." Myra lifted both hands like she was innocent of delivering the information. "Someone in HR knows someone. She's been with him for like eight months."

I sat back in my chair and looked across the office to where Deja was still at her computer, completely unaware that I was currently putting her entire situation together in my head. All those times Trey came hovering around her desk. Was that for show? Was that him making sure she felt comfortable? Or was that him doing what Trey did, which was be Trey regardless of who was watching?

"That's not my business," I finally said.

"Oop," Myra said. "I'm just saying."

"Tool my concern now." I grabbed my bag and stood up.

We talked the whole way to the parking garage with me telling her about Destin, about Tool's comments, about the fact that I was not ready for a ring even though I was absolutely crazy about that man. Myra thought I was overthinking it. I thought she needed to mind her business. We were both right.

I was still on the phone with her, sitting in my car in my own driveway, when my other line lit up.

Tool.

"Girl, hold on—" I switched over. "Hey, baby."

"Hey, beautiful. You off?"

"Just got home. I was on the phone with Myra."

"Tell her I said what's up. Don't stay on too long; I'm taking you to dinner tonight if you don't have Saviour."

I smiled. "Sacavè's dropping him off after school today."

"So I got you for about an hour?"

"Maybe two. Depending on traffic and how long Sacavè wants to stand on my porch."

He laughed. "A'ight. Call me when you're ready."

I switched back over to Myra. "That was Tool."

"I know. Finish what you were saying—"

"No, I'll talk to you tomorrow. He's taking me to dinner."

"Kia."

"Myra."

She made a sound. I laughed and hung up.

***

Sacavè pulled up about forty minutes later. I saw his car from the window and opened the door before Saviour could ring the bell seventeen times.

"Mommy." Saviour came in hot, bookbag hanging off one shoulder, something orange smeared near his mouth that I was choosing not to investigate yet.

"Hey, baby. Go put your bag in your room and wash your hands."

"Can I have a snack?"

"After you wash your hands."

"Okay." He ran past me and thundered up the stairs.

Sacavè was still on the porch. I didn't invite him in, but I left the door open, which was as much as I was giving.

"He eat?" I asked.

"Had a snack at three. He's good." Sacavè's eyes moved past me into the house briefly, then came back.

"I got a trip in a few weeks."

Something shifted in his face. He kept it together, but I saw it. "Again?"

"Yeah."

"I'm just saying, you're gone a lot."

"I'm gone sometimes," I said. "There's a difference."

"Saviour notices," he said.

There it was. I felt the conversation turning before he even finished the sentence. I knew that pivot. I had heard it enough times to recognize it in the first few words.

"Saviour is fine," I said evenly. "He talks to me every day when I'm gone, and when I'm here I'm fully here. Don't do that."

"I'm not doing anything." He paused. "I'm just asking. Maybe it makes more sense for him to be with me full time. Since you're—"

"Since I'm what, Sacavè?" I folded my arms. "Say it."

He looked at me. "Since it seems like you got other priorities right now."

"I have a son that I raise full time. I have a job. I have a life." I kept my voice low because Saviour was somewhere in the house. "I don't deserve vacations? I can't take trips?"

"You never wanted to go anywhere with me," he said.

"That's because you never planned anything," I said. "Tool handles everything. All I have to do is show up. You never had that in you."

Sacavè shook his head and looked out toward the street.

"Thought so," I said.

He didn't respond to that. And in the silence, I found myself actually looking at him, really looking, not with anger, not with whatever leftover hurt still lived in the corners of this situation, just looking. And I thought about Tool. About how different they were in ways that went deeper than what they did or didn't plan.

Tool grew up watching his parents do this together. Both of them in the house, both of them showing up, his father planning things and his mother letting herself be taken care of, and the two of them building something that lasted longer than he had been alive. He was the only boy, raised around that example every single day of his life. He knew what it looked like because he had seen it.

Sacavè didn't have that. Single mom, holding everything together by herself, love that came in the form of sacrifice and survival because that was what was available. He didn't have a blueprint for reciprocity. He had a blueprint for endurance, and he had handed me that same dynamic and called it a marriage.

And then I thought about Saviour. About what blueprint I was handing him right now. Whether watching his parents live separate lives in separate houses was going to show up somewhere in him fifteen, twenty years from now. Whether he knew how to let someone take care of him, or whether he only knew how to carry everything alone.

I didn't have an answer to that. I didn't think there was a clean one.

"Sacavè," I said, softer than the rest of the conversation. "I'm not going anywhere. I'm his mother. That doesn't change because I took a trip."

He nodded once. Slow. "I know."

"We good?"

He looked at me for a moment. "Yeah," he said. "We good."

He knocked twice on the door frame and called inside. "Aye, little man. See you this weekend."

“See you later, Daddy,” Saviour’s voice came flying down the stairs.

Sacavè walked back to his car without another word. Then Saviour appeared at my elbow with both hands held up for inspection.

“They clean,” he announced.

I looked down at him. “Let me see.” I turned his hands over. “What did you eat at school?”

“Nothing.”

“Saviour.”

“Some chips.”

I shook my head. “Come on. Let’s find you a real snack.”

Chapter 5

Sacavé

"So what are you looking for now?" the realtor asked.

"Three-bedroom max. Me, my son, and a guest room," I answered.

I might as well downsize. Four rooms don't really make sense for one person, plus I'm tired of Kia bringing up how I had Sena in the home we used to share. Every time she said it, it landed the same way, not because she was wrong, but because she wasn't, and I didn't have nothing to say back to it. With these divorce papers filed for real and processing, it's no hope for what we had. So fuck it. I'm cool with something simple for just me and my son. No stairs, no extra space just sitting there reminding me of what used to fill it. Something clean. Something that was only ours going forward.

"Same area?" she asked.

"Yeah, or near Forest Park," I agreed.

I wouldn't mind being closer to Kia. It's convenient for pickups and drop-offs, and Saviour's school is in that area too. It's further away from my job, but I'll manage. The commute wasn't the priority. My son was the priority, and cutting time off either end of that drive meant more time with him. I would take that trade every time.

"How soon you looking to sell?" she probed.

"ASAP. If I can secure a new spot, I'll move in there and put this on the market," I said.

"I can definitely work on both," she said, batting them long-ass lashes.

I couldn't help but feel hopeless in the relationship department. It felt to me like nothing was out there. Like all these women wanted was a nigga with money they could spend. You start talking to somebody these days and all of a sudden, soon as you enter their life, it starts falling apart, rent due, hair needs to be done, something always coming up right on time. Don't get me wrong, a nigga got paper. But my woman got to have her own motion too.

When I was a pharmacist, shit was different. This clean money that I actually got to put in work for ain't getting spent just anywhere. Most definitely not no oversized-ass and titties like my realtor; that shit just too fucking much. Nigga don't even want to be behind all that, gotta worry about whether it get wiped or washed properly. The woman is beautiful though, no question, like Naomi Campbell, but then add extra shit in her lips, too much ass, not enough thighs, big titties, and them overgrown fans on her eyelids.

I guess I should've done right by Kia if I wanted my dream girl.

She kept it professional though, shifted gears and walked me through the selling price for the home, what needed to be done to prepare it for the market, and started pulling up options for what a downsize could look like in the areas I mentioned. She knew her shit. I sat there half-listening, half-sitting in the weight of the fact that I was actually doing this shit, selling the house I bought thinking it was going to be the foundation of something that lasted. Picked it out together. Signed together. Brought Saviour home to it.

Then she looked up from her tablet and her voice got a little softer.

"I'm sorry your marriage didn't work out," she said. "You guys seemed so happy when I sold you your current home."

I nodded. Didn't say much back because there wasn't much to say. She was right. We were happy or something close enough to it that nobody on the outside could tell the difference. And I had made the choices I made and burned through all of that, and now I was sitting in front of the same woman who handed us the keys trying to figure out how fast I could move out. Wasn't nobody's fault but mine to carry.

"It is what it is," I said.

She nodded and left it there. I appreciated that.

We wrapped up the meeting with showings lined up, somebody coming to walk through my place by end of the week. It was in motion now. I walked out to my truck feeling lighter than I expected and heavier than I wanted to, the way you feel when something you been putting off finally just starts moving without you.

***

I pulled up to Saviour's school right at dismissal and sat in the pickup line with the music low. Watched the doors until they opened and kids started coming out. I spotted him before he saw me, bookbag bouncing, head swinging both ways scanning for my truck. Then he found it and his whole face changed. Came running full speed, climbed in, and dropped that bookbag on the floor.

"We getting a new house," I told him once we were pulling out.

He got still. "A new house?"

"Yeah. Just for me and you when you stay with Daddy."

He thought about it for a second. I could see him working through it, stacking questions. "What about our house?"

"We gon' sell it."

"Why can't you and Mommy and me just all live in the same house?" he asked.

I kept my eyes on the road. "Because Mommy got her house and Daddy getting his house. That's just how it is now, man. But we both still got you. That part don't change."

He looked out the window. Quiet for a minute. Then he asked, "Can I pick my room?"

"Yeah, you can pick your room."

"Can it be big?"

"Bigger than what you got now."

That was all he needed. He pulled out his iPad and that was the end of it. Just like that. Kids could set something heavy down and walk away from it in a way grown people spent years trying to learn. He would pick it back up eventually; I knew that. But right now he was good, and watching him let it go that easy did something to me I didn't have words for yet.

I thought about what she said the whole ride home. *You guys seemed so happy.*

We were. That was the honest truth of it. Kia was a good woman. Still is. I just hadn't been what she needed in the ways that actually mattered, and by the time I started to understand the difference, it was already too late. That was mine to carry. I wasn't running from it.

But something else had been sitting with me quiet lately. Something that felt less like grief and more like a door cracking open. The papers processing. A new address coming. Starting to feel like myself again in a way I hadn't in a long time.

With a nigga really back on the market, I'm ready to act like it.

Chapter 6

I don't know what I expected when Tool said Destin, but it wasn't this.

We pulled up to the hotel and I sat in the passenger seat for a second just looking at it. Right on the water. The kind of place that had its own smell, salt air, money, and a lobby that made you feel like you had been living wrong everywhere else. He had done it again. Every time I thought I had a ceiling on what this man was capable of, he came back and raised it.

"You good?" he asked, watching me look.

"You did this on purpose," I said.

He smiled. "I told you I was making it memorable."

We checked in and the room wasn't a room, it was a suite, and the balcony sat right over the Gulf. Turquoise water so clear it looked fake, white sand stretching out in both directions. I walked straight to the railing and just stood there. Four days. We had four whole days of this, and I wasn't wasting a single one of them.

***

The second night, he did something with the room while I was in the shower. I came out wrapped in a towel and stopped in the doorway. Rose petals. Candles. Champagne on ice and a little box sitting on the table that my eyes went to and then snapped away from just as fast.

"Tool—"

"It's not a ring," he said, reading me. He was leaning against the balcony door with his arms folded, dressed nice, looking at me like I was something he had been waiting a long time to see. "Calm down."

I exhaled. "Okay."

"Come here."

I walked over slow, towel still on, completely underdressed for whatever this was. He opened the box before I could reach for it, a bracelet, simple and beautiful, something that said he paid attention to what I actually liked and not just what was expensive.

"I'm not asking you to marry me," he said. "I'm asking you to be my girlfriend. Officially. I want you to be mine, Kia."

I looked at him. At the room. At everything he had put together just to ask me something most men asked in a text message, if they asked at all. And I felt it, the *yes* sitting right there, ready, and then the other thing came up right behind it.

"I'm still legally married," I said.

He nodded like he had been expecting that. "I know."

"That's not me stalling or making excuses. I just—" I sat on the edge of the bed. "It don't feel right to say I'm somebody's girlfriend when I'm still technically somebody's wife. Even if it's just paperwork at this point."

"How much longer?" he asked. He wasn't frustrated; he was just asking.

"A few more months. Maybe less, depending on how smooth it goes."

He was quiet for a second. Then he walked over, took the bracelet out of the box, and put it on my wrist himself, clasping it like it was already decided.

"Then I'll ask you again when you're officially single," he said.

"Tool—"

"I'm not going nowhere." He tilted my chin up. "I just want you to know what I'm asking for. So when that day comes, it's not a surprise."

I looked at him. This man. This patient, intentional, ridiculous man.

"Okay," I said quietly.

"Okay," he said back. And then he smiled and the whole weight of the moment shifted into something lighter. "Now go put some clothes on. I made reservations."

***

We packed four days full like we were trying to fit a month in. Jet skis in the morning, him showing off, me screaming and laughing and holding on for my life. A sunset dolphin cruise where we actually saw them and I grabbed his arm like a kid. Shopping on the strip, he bought things for me before I could reach for my wallet, which I had stopped arguing about somewhere between Puerto Rico and now. We ate good every night, different restaurants, the kind of meals you talked about after. We rented bikes one afternoon and rode the whole stretch of the beach road until my legs gave up and he laughed at me the whole way back.

***

We were at dinner the last night right on the water, candles on the table and music low in the background.

"I want you to meet my family," he said.

I looked up from my plate. "Yeah?"

"Yeah. My mom, my dad, my sisters." He said it easy, like it wasn't a big deal, but I knew it was.

"I want that," I said. "I definitely want to meet the people responsible for making and raising a man like you."

For a split second, the cool, composed version of Tool, the one who always had a plan and a smirk ready, just evaporated. Something moved across his face, something raw and unguarded that made my chest tighten. It was pride mixed with a kind of soft, deep-rooted love I hadn't seen him show for anything else yet. His eyes searched mine, looking for a second like that little boy he used to be, before he pulled it back together. "They gon' love you," he said, his voice dropping an octave, thick with a certainty that made me believe him.

"You don't know that."

"I do." He reached across the table and covered my hand with his. "I know everything I need to know."

We sat in that moment for a minute. The water, the candles, the comfortable quiet that had become one of my favorite things about being with him. Then he opened his mouth and what came out wasn't what either of us expected.

"I love you."

He stopped. I watched it register on his face, the slip, the realness of it, the fact that he couldn't take it back, and something in his expression said he didn't want to.

I didn't say anything right away. Just looked at him.

"Kia—"

"I love you too," I said.

He exhaled like he had been holding something. "Yeah?"

"I've been feeling it for a while," I admitted. "I just didn't want to say it too soon and have it be one of those things that's out there before it's ready."

"It's ready," he said.

"I know."

He shook his head slow, smiling at the table. "I've been in love with you since the first time I saw you," he said. "I know how that sounds."

"How does it sound?"

"Like something a nigga says." He looked up. "But I mean it. First time. Something just told me."

I believed him because I thought about how he had moved from the beginning. The patience. The consistency. The way nothing about his approach ever felt like a game. He had known something before I caught up to it, and he had just waited.

"You should've said something sooner," I said.

"You weren't ready sooner."

He was right. And I loved him for knowing that too.

***

He waited until dessert to hit me with the next one.

"You want more kids?"

I looked up. "Right now?"

"Not right now right now." He leaned back in his chair. "Just in general. Down the line."

I thought about it honestly. "I don't know. Maybe. Saviour's at a good age and I'm not opposed to it. Why?"

"Because I don't have any and I want some," he said. "Not tomorrow. But it's something I think about."

"How many?"

"At least one. Maybe two."

I nodded slow. Filed that away. "Okay."

"*Okay* 'it's a conversation' or *okay*—"

"*Okay* 'it's a conversation'," I said. "A real one. But not tonight. Tonight I want dessert and then I want to ride that Ferris wheel."

He laughed. "The SkyWheel?"

"Whatever it's called. The big Ferris wheel looking thing. I want to do it."

"You barely made it on the flight to and from PR."

"I'll be fine if you're with me."

He flagged down the waiter.

***

I was not fine.

I was gripping his arm with both hands by the time we got to the top, eyes wide, refusing to look down while he sat there calm as ever, looking out at the water like we were on a park bench.

"It's beautiful up here," he said.

"I will hurt you," I said.

He put his arm around me and I buried my face in his shoulder, and he laughed that whole deep laugh that I had decided was one of my favorite sounds. By the time we came back around to the bottom I was laughing too, that shaky kind that comes after your heart rate drops.

"I want to call Saviour," I said when we stepped off, still catching my breath.

"Yeah, call him," Tool said.

I dialed and Sacavè picked up first, told me Saviour was already in the bath, but a minute later I heard the little feet and then his voice.

"Mommy. Did you have fun?"

"So much fun, baby. You good?"

"Yes. Daddy let me stay up."

"Of course he did."

Tool was standing next to me, close enough to hear, and Saviour must've heard something because he said, "Is Tool there?"

I glanced over. "Yeah, he's here."

"Hi, Tool." He yelled it loud enough that Tool heard it without the phone even being near him.

Tool leaned in a little. "What's up, little man?"

"I miss you," Saviour said.

I felt something shift in my chest. Tool went still for just a second, then said, "I miss you too, man. I'll see you when we get back, a'ight?"

"Okay. Bring me something."

"Saviour—" I started.

"I got him," Tool said, smiling.

I got off the phone a few minutes later and we walked back toward the hotel, his hand in mine. I was quiet and he let me be quiet, which was another thing I loved about him.

I hadn't realized how much time Tool had been putting in with Saviour. Most days after school, I knew he came around, I knew they played together, kicked the ball in the backyard, watched TV while I worked. It was sweet, like it was part of this thing Tool and I were building. I hadn't registered that Saviour had built something of his own with him. Something that was his, separate from me. Something that made him miss Tool when he was at his daddy's.

That sat with me. Not because it was bad. But because it was real in a way I hadn't prepared for. My son was attached.

***

We spent the last morning slow. Room service, balcony, no plans. Just sitting with it before we had to let it go. I was already dreading going back, not to Saviour, never to Saviour, but to the noise of regular life that had a way of making everything feel more complicated than it needed to be.

"You good?" he asked, same question he always asked, already knowing.

"Yeah," I said. "Just not ready to leave."

"We'll come back."

"Promise?"

He looked at me. "I don't say things I don't mean."

I believed that too. I believed all of it. That was maybe the newest thing, getting used to being with somebody and not waiting for the other shoe. Not scanning for the thing that was going to change it. Just believing him, because he had given me every reason to and not one reason not to.

We drove home with the windows down and the music up and his hand on my thigh the whole way, and I thought about love at first sight and patience and a little boy who said *I miss you* like it was the easiest thing in the world, and somewhere on that drive I stopped waiting for something to go wrong and just let it be good.

Chapter 7

4 Months Later

"My decree is here," I said into the phone.

I was on FaceTime with Tamia, and she started screaming before I could even finish the sentence.

"Finally. Let me see it," she yelled, already moving her face closer to her camera like she was going to be able to read it through mine.

I ripped open the envelope. My hands were moving faster than my brain. There it was. Official court seal. Legal language I skimmed over because none of the middle part mattered. And at the bottom in block letters: DECREE OF DIVORCE – FINAL.

"I'm officially divorced," I said, my voice barely above a whisper.

"How you feel, sista?" Tamia asked, her voice dropping to match mine.

"Free," I said.

And I meant it. Not bitter free, not relieved free like something bad was finally over. Just free. Like I had been carrying something so long I had forgotten what my own shoulders felt like without the weight, and now I was standing up straight for the first time in years.

We talked for a while after that. All the things that came with it, the name change process, updating my license, my social security card, my bank accounts, every piece of ID that still said *Sanders* on it. Tamia had a friend who had done it recently and walked me through what to expect. It was more paperwork, more steps, more of the administrative weight of undoing a life you had built with somebody. But I didn't mind any of it. Every form was one more thing that put distance between who I was and who I used to be trying to be.

After we hung up, I sat on my couch staring at the paper for a long time. Just me and the quiet and that court seal.

It was official. I was Kia Williams again.

My phone buzzed. *Tool.*

Tool: *How was your day, beautiful?*

I smiled and texted back: *Amazing. My divorce is final.*

Three dots popped up. Then disappeared. Then my phone rang.

"Say that again," he said as soon as I answered.

"My divorce is final. Papers came today," I said, grinning.

"We celebrating tonight. Be dressed by eight; I'm taking you out," he said. No hesitation. Like he had been waiting on this day same as me.

"Baby, it's a Wednesday. And I got Saviour—"

"Call your mama or I can ask one of my sisters. You need to celebrate. Tonight is about you," he said.

"Okay," I agreed, because honestly, I wanted to celebrate too. I had earned this. We both had.

***

Hours later, I was standing in front of my mirror in a sleek red dress. My mama had already come to pick up Saviour, and Tool was at my door with flowers. Pink roses, like always. Never had to tell him twice.

"There's my free woman," he said, pulling me into a hug as I walked out.

"Officially single," I said against his chest.

"Not for long," he whispered into my hair.

I pulled back and looked at him. He was already smiling. I let it go for tonight.

He took me to *Canoe*, this upscale restaurant sitting right on the Chattahoochee River. I had heard about it but never been there. The kind of place where the ambiance did half the work, water visible through the windows, lighting low and warm, the kind of quiet that meant everything on the menu was going to be worth it.

"To new beginnings," Tool said, raising his glass.

"To new beginnings," I echoed, and we clinked glasses. The relief. The gratitude. The strange, particular joy of sitting across from the right person on the night the wrong chapter finally closed.

We ordered, salmon for me, steak for him, and somewhere between the bread basket and the entrées, the conversation found its way there.

"So what you wanna do now that you free?" Tool asked, cutting into his steak, watching me casual.

"Honestly? I just wanna keep doing what we been doing. Being happy," I said.

"What about marriage?" he asked, watching my face careful now.

I paused, fork halfway to my mouth. "I don't know."

"I'm not saying right now. I'm just asking in general," he said.

I set my fork down. Thought about how to say it honest without saying it wrong. "To be honest? I don't think I ever wanna get married again."

Something flickered across his face. Quick. He put it away just as fast, but I saw it. He picked his glass up and took a sip, and when he set it back down he said, "Well. I'm a man of my word."

"I know," I said.

And I did know. That was what made the moment sit heavy. Because he had told me many times that he was going to give me his last name. The energy shifted after that. Not cold, not ruined. Just different. Like he was recalibrating something quietly on his side of the table while we finished our food.

***

After dinner we walked around downtown, the night air cool and easy, his hand in mine. We had been quiet in that comfortable way for a few minutes when he stopped walking and turned to me.

"You remember my question in Destin?" Tool said.

"Yes," I said.

"And your answer," he continued, looking at me.

"Yes," I said. "I'm your girlfriend."

"Been that, huh," he said, pulling me close with a half-smile that meant he already knew.

"Been that," I confirmed.

He kissed me right there on the sidewalk, slow and sure, and I melted into it the way I always did with him, like my body had decided it trusted him before my mind had finished making up its own.

When he pulled back, he was still close. "So which date is our official anniversary? Today, or when I first asked in Destin?"

I loved that he cared about that. I loved that it mattered to him enough to ask. Me and Sacavè never really had a date; we met, started kicking it, he started calling me his girl and I went with it, counted the years from somewhere approximate that neither of us could agree on anyway. It was never that intentional. This was different.

"From Destin for sure," I said. "You asked with so much intention then. Even though I was yours before that."

He nodded like that was the right answer. Like he already knew what he was going to put in his phone.

***

We ended up at his place. And I don't know if it was the dress or the wine, but the night moved the way nights did with us when we had nowhere to be and nothing to prove. Slow at first, his hands finding me in the low light, everything unhurried. And then less slow. And then not slow at all. He knew my body the way you know something you've been paying close attention to, knew what made me hold my breath and what made me say his name, and by the time it was over, I was somewhere between satisfied and undone in the best possible way.

I fell asleep in his bed with his arm around me and didn't move until morning.

***

I felt his lips on my forehead before I was fully awake. Then my temple. Then my cheek.

"Baby." His voice was low, still morning-rough. "I'm heading out to work. Treat this like it's yours. Your key's on the table."

I opened one eye. He was already dressed, looking entirely too put together for whatever time it was.

"I'll take an Uber," I said, my voice still half-asleep.

"Take my truck. Just come pick me up when you get off. I'll ride the clock until you pull up."

He looked at me for a second. Then he leaned down and kissed me again. "Okay."

That was it. No back-and-forth, no making it complicated. Just *okay*. That was one of the most attractive things about him, the thing I kept coming back to every time I tried to put words to what made him different. He was forward-thinking in a way that made everything feel manageable. Like there was always a solution and he was already three steps ahead looking for it. Something about that turned me on. It wasn't just the romance; it was the steadiness. The problem solving.

The way he moved through life like he had already decided nothing was going to knock him off course.

I listened to the door close and pulled his covers up around me and fell back into his scent and his sheets and slept like I hadn't slept in years.

***

My 10 AM alarm went off like a personal attack.

I laid there for a solid five minutes negotiating with myself before I rolled out of bed and stood in the middle of his room blinking. That's when I remembered: I had nothing here but a red dress, heels, and last night's makeup.

I looked at the dress on the chair. Looked at myself in his mirror. I went to his dresser.

I found a T-shirt and some shorts, put them on, looked at myself again, and sent him a text with a picture attached: *Guess I'll be you today.*

He responded fast: *Ha. Not bad for me.*

I got home and clocked in from my home office right on time. The morning moved steady, calls, emails, nothing that required more from me than I had to give. I was still floating a little from the night before. Divorce final, anniversary official, woke up in that man's bed feeling like somebody had reset something in me.

At 3 PM, my phone buzzed.

Sacavè: *stop sucking dick, your son just got out of school.*

I opened the garage without responding. He was earlier than normal anyway, and I was already on a call and couldn't give him the reaction I wanted to, so I gave him nothing instead. That was worse anyway, and he knew it.

Saviour knew the routine by now: office door was off-limits until 8 PM. So, when I heard the office door and then the particular energy of somebody moving through my house who was not my son, I already knew. I kept my eyes on my screen and my voice level.

"Yes, ma'am, my pleasure," I said, and waited until she hung up before I swung around in my chair.

Sacavè was standing in my office doorway.

"Text my phone with some respect or don't text it at all," I said, standing up and walking toward him.

He looked me over slow. Clocked the T-shirt. Clocked the truck in the driveway. Something moved behind his eyes before he got it under control.

"You got on this nigga clothes and his truck in your driveway," he said, keeping his voice low. "Let me guess, he in your room sleep?"

"No," I said. "He's at work."

I smiled when I said it. I couldn't help it.

"Did you bust in here hoping to see him having me bent over the table?" I pushed past him into the hallway. "*Saviourrr.*"

Saviour came running from the back, bookbag still on, sneakers squeaking on the floor.

"Hey, son, how was school?" I said, pulling him into a hug.

"Good. Where's Tool, Mommy?" he asked, eyes already scanning past me.

Sacavè made a sound with his teeth.

"He asked because he saw his truck," I said, not looking at Sacavè. Then to Saviour: "He's at work, baby. You'll see him later. You got homework?"

Saviour nodded.

"Go start on it please."

He trotted off down the hall and I turned back around. Sacavè was already moving, opening the door to the half bath, glancing into the living room, moving toward the stairs with the specific energy of a man who was looking for something he was hoping not to find and also kind of hoping to find.

I watched him from the bottom of the stairs and laughed. I couldn't hold it.

"Sacavè."

He stopped.

"He's not here," I said. "You can stop looking."

He came back down the stairs slow. Stood in the foyer with his jaw tight, not quite ready to leave but out of reasons to stay.

"So did you receive your decree yesterday too?" I asked.

He looked at me. "What's that?"

"The document that says the divorce is final," I said.

Sacavè squinted. Something settled over his face that wasn't anger and wasn't sadness and was somehow both. "A'ight. So that's it then."

"Yup," I said.

"You happy now, right?" he asked. The words came out quieter than I think he meant them to, and underneath them was something he was trying not to show.

"Don't do that," I said.

He nodded once. "I'm out." He moved toward the door.

"Sacavè, wait."

"What, Kia?" he asked, hand on the door, not fully turning back.

I waited for a second. "I hope you know this don't change nothing with Saviour. You're still his father. That won't change."

He was quiet for a second.

"I know that much," he said. "I ain't never gon' stop showing up for mine."

He walked out and pulled the door behind him. I stood in the foyer and listened to his car start and pull away.

I looked down at the T-shirt I was wearing. Tool's name wasn't on it. Didn't need to be.

I went upstairs to check on Saviour.

Chapter 8

Sacavè

I made it two blocks before I had to pull over.

I sat there in my truck on the side of the road with both hands still on the wheel and the engine running, staring at nothing. The divorce is final. I knew it was coming. Had known for months it was coming. But knowing something is coming and having it actually arrive are two different things, and right now my chest felt like something in it had finally given out after holding too long.

I wanted to call somebody.

I pulled out my phone and just held it. Scrolled without thinking. My thumb hovered over Sena's name and I sat there looking at it.

Fucking Sena.

She did this. Set it in motion, signed what she had no business signing, made decisions that wasn't hers to make. And she was still in my phone. Still the first person I reached for when I didn't know what else to do, because that's what years of friendship does; it makes somebody a reflex even after they become the reason you're sitting on the side of the road falling apart.

What was I even going to say? *Thanks?*

I don't know how to feel. Don't know who to call or how to process what was sitting on me right now. Kia had looked so unbothered. That almost hurt worse than everything else, not because I wanted her to be miserable, but because she was real content. Glowing. Had that nigga's truck in her driveway and his clothes on and my son asking where he was like it was the most natural thing in the world.

She had moved on. Fully. Completely. In a way that made it clear she wasn't looking back.

I sat there until the feeling passed enough for me to drive. Then I pulled off and took the long way home.

The week moved slow the way weeks did when you had too much time inside your own head. I went to work, picked up Saviour, dropped him off at Kia's, came home, worked out, went to sleep, did it again. Kept myself busy enough not to sit still too long.

Friday couldn't come fast enough.

***

"Daddy, can we get pizza?" Saviour asked from the backseat the second he climbed in from school.

"Yeah, we can do that. What you want on it?" I asked.

"Just cheese," he said, like that was obvious, like any other answer would've been crazy.

Every weekend, Saviour was with me. Friday after school straight through to Sunday evening. That was our routine and I never missed it, not once, not for anything. It didn't matter how bad the week had been, how inside my head I was, how many times I had driven past that house on purpose or replayed conversations I should've let go. Friday at 3:15, I was in that pickup line and I was put together. My son didn't need to carry any of that. He just needed his dad.

We hit *Blaze Pizza*, got his cheese and my pepperoni, and sat down in the restaurant like two people with nowhere to be and all the time in the world.

"And then Marcus said his dad could beat up everybody's dad," Saviour said, completely serious, pizza grease on his chin. "And I said, not my daddy."

I looked at him. "Fucking right," I said, dapping him up.

"Daddy." He pointed at me. "Bad word."

"My bad. You right," I said, straightening my face. "That was a bad word. Don't repeat it."

"I know," he said, already back on his pizza, completely unbothered.

I watched him eat and felt everything from the week just . . . fall off. That was what he did. Didn't know he did it, wasn't trying to. But something about sitting across from my son in a pizza restaurant on a Friday, watching him chew with his whole face, just reset something in me that nothing else could touch.

***

Back at the crib, we played *Madden.* Well, I played *Madden.* Saviour sat next to me with the controller that wasn't plugged into anything, fully convinced he was running the same game I was.

"Daddy, did you see that? I scored," he yelled, jumping up.

"I saw, man. That was clean." I said, dapping him up again.

He sat back down satisfied and went right back to pressing buttons on a dead controller like he was about to take it to the championship.

I let him have every single point.

My phone buzzed on the coffee table. *Kia.*

Kia: *Can you drop Saviour off a little later on Sunday? I got somewhere to be.*

I read it twice. Put the phone down. Picked it back up.

Sacavè: *Yeah, that's cool.*

Kia: *Thanks.*

That was it. Short. Unbothered. She had somewhere to be on a Sunday and she needed an extra hour and she wasn't going to explain herself, and she didn't owe me one either. I knew that. I just sat with it for a second longer than I needed to before I set the phone back down and turned my attention back to the game.

Saviour scored again on his unplugged controller and lost his mind about it.

I dapped him up and kept playing.

***

The rest of the weekend was ours. Saturday morning, I let him sleep in, got him breakfast from *Mamie's Breakfast*, eggs, turkey bacon, toast, orange juice, and we ate in front of cartoons with no agenda. He told me about school, about Marcus and his daddy, about some dinosaur documentary his teacher showed them that he was convinced meant dinosaurs were coming back.

"They not coming back, son," I told him.

"But the teacher said the bones—"

"The bones been there. They not coming back."

He looked skeptical. I let him be skeptical.

After breakfast we ran some errands, stopped at the park for an hour, and that afternoon I took him to get a haircut. He sat in the chair serious as a grown man, watching himself in the mirror the whole time, telling the barber exactly what he wanted like he had been getting his hair cut for forty years.

"He yours?" the barber asked me, smiling.

"That's my boy," I said.

"He got your energy," he said.

I didn't say anything back. Just watched my son in that mirror.

On Sunday we watched movies, ordered wings, and I beat him in *Connect Four* six times before he flipped the board and said it was broken. I let that go too.

By Sunday evening I had him fed, bag packed, and fresh. I got him in the truck and headed toward Kia's.

Chapter 9

"I'm really nervous, baby," I said, looking at myself for the fiftieth time in the mirror. "What if they don't like me?"

"They're gonna love you," Tool said through the speaker. "They already love you from what I told them."

That should've helped. It didn't.

I had met somebody's people before, but never like this. Never a whole Sunday dinner put together specifically around meeting me. That was the part that had my stomach hurting. Casual run-ins were one thing; this was intentional. This was everybody in one place, eyes on me, forming opinions. I needed everything to be right. Outfit, right. Hair, right. First impression, right.

I looked at myself one more time and decided this was as good as it was going to get.

***

Tool hosted at his house. When I turned onto his street, I saw the cars before I even got to the driveway, nice ones, lining both sides, spilling into the cul-de-sac. I parked near the mailbox and texted him.

I'm here.

I sat there. Watched the three dots pop up and disappear. Pop up and disappear.

Nothing.

A minute passed. Then two. Then three. My nerves started filling in every second of silence with something worse than the last thing. *What if they already didn't like me and nobody had told Tool yet. What if—*

A *Jeep Cherokee* pulled up and I stopped spiraling long enough to watch. A slim, lanky man got out first, walked around, and opened the passenger door. A woman stepped out, short, plump, pretty. When she turned and we made eye contact, something clicked immediately. She had Tool's eyes. His nose. She favored him so strong.

The man opened the back door and two kids climbed out. When they turned around, I clocked the faces.

Nala. BJ.

"Ms. *Kiaaaaaa.*" Nala came running before I even had the door fully open, both arms out, *iPad* still somehow in one hand.

And just like that, every nervous bone in my body left. If this whole family was anything like this little girl, who had only met me once at Saviour's birthday party months ago and still ran to me like I was somebody she had been missing, I was going to be just fine.

"Hey, pretty girl," I said, hugging her down.

BJ walked over cool, gave me a side hug, a little nod. "Hi, Ms. Kia."

I waved a shy little wave over at their parents and walked toward them. "I'm Kia, Tool's—" I paused just half a second, "—girlfriend."

His sister reached out with both arms before I could even finish extending my hand. "Girl, we hug in this family unless you too boujee," she said, pulling me in. "I'm Tia. This is my husband Nard."

Nard hugged me too, like I wasn't a stranger at all.

The five of us walked up toward the front door together. Nala had my hand in one of hers and her *iPad* in the other, chattering about something the whole way up. BJ walked beside his dad scrolling his phone. Tia and Nard were hand-in-hand behind us. I noticed the easy way they moved together, comfortable, natural. Tool had grown up watching that. It showed in how he moved with me, and I hadn't fully put it together until right now.

I knocked at the door.

An older woman answered, petite, silver hair long and pretty, the kind of face that had been beautiful her whole life and knew it without being arrogant about it.

"Honeygram!" Nala dropped my hand and launched herself into the woman's arms.

Everybody moved around me and I stood there frozen in the doorway like my feet had forgotten what they were for.

"Come in, young lady. You must be Kia," she said, reaching for me. "We've been sitting in here watching to see if you were ever gonna get out of that darn car."

My mouth dropped open.

"Yeah, why didn't you use your key? That's what it's for," Tool said, appearing from somewhere behind her, grinning like he had been in on it the whole time.

"Don't do me like that," I said, laughing and slapping his arm.

He kissed my forehead. "I got you. Relax." Then he turned me toward her. "This is my grandma Ernestine. We call her Honeygram."

She pulled me into a hug that had no business being as strong as it was for how small she was.

Tool took my hand, fingers laced through mine, and walked me up to the living room. The whole room looked up.

"Y'all, this is Kia." He pointed around the room as he went. "That's Tank, my mom's older brother. Tajah, my little sister; Fidel, her boyfriend. Cool, my cousin. Toot, my youngest sister; Von, her husband. And Felicia, my dad's sister."

One by one, they got up and hugged me. Every single one. Tool had not been exaggerating when he said he was a hugger; this whole family was built that way. By the time the last person sat back down, I had been hugged seven times and my nerves were somewhere on the floor behind me.

Then Tool walked me into the kitchen.

“Ma. Pops,” he said. “This is Kia.”

I stepped forward, ready to hug them too.

His mother, Ms. Kristen, was beautiful in a quiet, refined way. Natural silver locs, smooth skin, the posture of a woman who had never moved through a room without intention. She stepped toward me and pressed her cheek to mine, then the other cheek. Air kisses.

His father reached out his hand.

A handshake.

I shook it and smiled and kept my face together, but something in the back of my mind registered the difference. The whole family had hugged me. His parents hadn’t. I kept that tucked away without reading too much into it. Ms. Kristen’s eyes were warm even if her greeting was measured. She was the kind of woman who formed her opinions on her own time, and I respected that even as it made me want to work a little harder. His father was quiet and watchful in the way that men who raised sons sometimes are, sizing up without being unkind about it. I understood that too.

***

The food was already done and it was everything. The dining room table looked like somebody had put real love and real hours into it: baked mac and cheese with the crust on top, fried chicken, candied yams, collard greens, cornbread, potato salad, green beans with smoked turkey, and a peach cobbler on the counter that I had already clocked three times since I walked through the door.

The kids ate downstairs. The adults filled the dining table and I ended up between Tool and Tia, which felt like exactly the right place to be. Tool’s hand stayed on my thigh the entire dinner.

"So I hear you have a son," Ms. Kristen said, looking at me pleasantly from across the table. "Saviour?"

"Yes, ma'am," I said.

"Where is he today?"

"He's with his father on weekends," I answered. "I texted his dad earlier to bring him back a little later tonight. I should've brought him; I didn't realize how many kids would be here. He would've loved it."

"Bring him next time," she said, and the way she said *next time* felt like it was already assumed there would be one.

The conversation moved around the table easy. Jokes, stories I was getting just enough context to follow, Felicia with her raspy voice that sounded like she smoked *Newports* all her life, Tank and Cool going back and forth about something football-related. I kept eating and listening and laughing.

"Alright, y'all," Tool said, and the table quieted a little. He glanced over at me first with a look I couldn't read. "I got a surprise for everybody."

Every head at the table turned toward me.

"Oh no," I said, covering my mouth because it was still full. "There won't be any of those coming for a while."

Everybody laughed.

I caught Ms. Kristen's face in the middle of it. The smile was there, but underneath it something passed between her and Tool's father, quick, private, a look that carried weight they weren't putting on the table today. I didn't know the full story behind it, but I took a mental note. Tool's expression for just a second said something too; not embarrassed, not bothered. Something quieter than that. Like a door he was keeping closed for now but hadn't forgotten was there.

"Yeah, nah, not yet," he said, laughing it off. "I'm talking about *Disney World*. Orlando, next month. I got an *Airbnb* big enough for fourteen. Stay's already secured. I'm thinking we do a Sprinter and drive unless everybody wants to do their own flights."

The energy shifted into something louder and more excited.

"Me and Nard, for sure. I don't mind doing flights," Tia said immediately.

"I'm down. Von's gonna be in Baltimore for work next month anyway," Toot said.

"Well, we'll tag along, use our points, stay in our own suite; that still leaves two spots at the *Airbnb*," Ms. Kristen said.

"I'll let the young folk have this one," Felicia said. "Count me in for the next cabin trip though. I like the outdoors."

"Same," Tank said.

"Same," Tajah and Fidel said together.

Ms. Kristen turned to me. "What about your family, baby? I'm sure you've got kids on your side too."

"Yes, ma'am, I have a niece and a nephew. My sister's kids."

"Well, sounds like we've got it figured out then," she said, and smiled at me like the matter was settled.

Tool squeezed my thigh under the table.

***

Conversation kept going, somebody brought up a trip somebody else had taken, Felicia had a story that took three detours before it got to the point, the cobbler came out and I had two servings and felt no shame about either one. She put her whole foot in there. At some point, I looked down at my watch.

"Can I excuse myself?" I asked. "I have to go meet my ex-husband to get Saviour."

"Of course, you're excused, baby," Ms. Kristen said.

Tool and I both got up from the table. He walked behind me with his hand at the small of my back, guiding me through the room, past the goodbye hugs from everyone again on the way out. When we got to my truck, he opened the door and stood there while I stepped up.

"So you like my family." Not really a question.

"I love them already," I said. "I love how welcoming they are. Every single one of them."

"Told you." He leaned against the door frame. "And they down for *Disney*."

I looked at him. "You actually booked it."

"I told you I was going to."

"You told me we were looking at stays—"

"And then I booked it," he said, unbothered, smiling.

We talked for a few more minutes in the driveway while the sun finished going down, him leaning in my window, me not really in a rush to pull off even though I needed to. Eventually I had to go.

"I'll call you when I get Saviour," I said.

"Drive safe," he said, and kissed me through the window before stepping back.

***

I was barely three minutes down the road when I picked up the phone.

"Girl," I said the second Tamia answered.

"What happened?"

"I just left Tool's family dinner."

"And?"

"Tamia." I paused for effect. "I love every single one of them."

She screamed. I laughed.

"Okay, okay, okay, tell me everything," she said.

I ran through all of it, Honeygram watching me sit in the truck, Nala running to me in the cul-de-sac, the food, the table, Ms. Kristen with her air kisses, all of it. Tamia was reacting to every piece of it in real time.

"Oh . . . and listen," I said, turning onto the highway. "Tool announced at dinner that he booked *Disney World* for next month. Big *Airbnb*, the whole family's going, and they asked about bringing family on my side." I paused. "So."

Silence.

"Girl, I do not have *Disney* money."

"*Disney World*?" Brielle's voice shot through the background loud and clear.

"What did I say about staying out of my conversation when I'm on the phone?" Tamia said away from the receiver.

I was cracking up.

"Sis, Tool already got the *Airbnb*. We just figuring out if we're driving or flying. It's gonna work out," I said.

"Kia—"

"Tamia."

She exhaled. I could hear her thinking through it. "I'm not making any promises."

"I'm not asking for promises. I'm asking you to show up."

She was quiet for a second. "What are the dates?"

I was still laughing when I pulled into my neighborhood. Sacavè's car was already in the driveway; him and Saviour stood outside.

I told Tamia I would call her back.

Chapter 10

Sacavè

When we pulled up, Tool's truck wasn't there. Good. I didn't feel like dealing with all that today.

"Come on, son," I said, helping Saviour out the car.

We knocked a couple of times. No answer. We were walking back to the truck when Kia pulled in. She hopped out looking good, too good. Hair freshly done, outfit casual but put together. Like she wasn't trying, but she was.

She opened the garage and bent down before she even acknowledged me.

"Hey, baby," she said, pulling Saviour in.

"Hi, Mommy. Me and Daddy had so much fun," Saviour said.

"That's good, baby. I love your haircut, let me see." She spun him by his shoulders. "*Nice*. Okay, go upstairs for a sec; let me talk to Daddy."

Saviour ran inside and I stood there in the driveway with my hands in my pockets.

"What's up?" I asked.

"You wanna come in? We beefin'?" she asked.

"I'm chillin'," I said.

I couldn't fake it. Couldn't stand in her kitchen and make small talk like I didn't feel some type of way about all of this. The divorce was final. She'd moved on. New nigga. And she was standing in front of me looking like that, and I had nothing going that came close to her. Every woman I had entertained since we been done felt like a cheap imitation, a placeholder that only served to remind me of the original. I wasn't just comparing them to her. I was losing to her.

"Sooo," she said. "I want you to take Saviour to *Disney* next month."

"Cool. Set it up, let me know how much you need," I said.

"The trip is already planned and paid for," she said.

I looked at her. "What that mean?"

"It's with my boyfriend and his family."

Something in my chest tightened. "Oh, nah. I'm cool. This ain't that."

"I wasn't inviting you or anything," she said. "I was telling you I plan on taking Saviour."

"So you don't care about me asking you to keep him away from your situation?" I said.

"Did you forget you had Sena around our son?" she asked.

"You never said you ain't want Saviour around her. Not once," I said. "I don't want my son feeling the worst end of this divorce. That's all I'm saying."

"And he won't. Tool is good with him. Saviour likes him."

"It's *Disney World*," I said, and the words came out flatter than I meant them to. "I know my son gone like it. I ain't gone give you a hard time about it." I paused. "But I want my wishes about him respected. And I want to experience shit with my son too. I should be the one taking him to *Disney*."

"Then plan something," she said, like it was simple.

"Kia—"

"These trips I've been on have been planned by him. Everything. All I have to do is show up." She stopped herself. "You just . . . you don't put in the effort. That's why we didn't wo—" She cut herself off. Looked away. "Never mind. Just plan something, Sacavè."

I scoffed. "Cool."

She turned and walked inside. I turned and walked to my truck. Got in. Sat there. Then I hit the steering wheel.

We didn't work because I didn't plan shit?

Is that what it came down to? Four years of marriage and that was the summary? I turned the ignition and pulled off and sat with that the whole drive home.

***

When I got home, I went straight to the stack of old mail I had been meaning to sort through since the move. Took me twenty minutes of digging before I found it. The counselor who had worked with me and Kia about two years back.

I wasn't the type to go looking for somebody to sit across from and talk about my feelings. But I also wasn't the type to keep running into the same wall and act surprised about it. Something wasn't working inside me and I was tired of not knowing what it was.

Tonight I needed something else. I was frustrated and I needed to let something off. So I texted my favorite eater.

I had met shorty about six months back. Cool girl. Uncomplicated in the best possible way, she didn't want anything from me except the same thing I wanted from her. Juicier than what I usually went for but it wasn't sloppy. She had a ring on her finger that I peeped the first time and never asked about. Wasn't my business. She didn't ask about my situation either. That was the agreement without it ever being said out loud.

Sacavè: *You free tonight?*

Shorty: *I gotta figure out how I'm getting away,* she texted back.

An hour later, her car pulled up.

"What you had to get away from?" I asked when she stepped out.

"Family dinner my big brother had," she said, tucking her keys away.

I lifted her hand, looked at the ring. Big. Nice. "You married?"

"Not happily," she said, and walked past me toward the door.

I let it go and followed her inside.

***

She took her time with me. That was her thing; she wasn't in a rush, never had been, moved like she was enjoying herself and wanted me to know it. By the time she was done, I was somewhere between unconscious and grateful. She cleaned up in the bathroom, came back out put together, and kissed me on the cheek.

"I gotta go," she said.

"A'ight," I said.

I watched her pull out of the driveway from the window and then went to the shower.

Hot water, steam, nothing to do but think. And my brain went exactly where I didn't want it to go. I stood there wondering if that was how it had started with Tool and Kia. I turned the water up hotter and tried to shake it loose. It didn't fully work. But I got out, dried off, and kept moving because that was the only option.

***

I was on my lunch break when I finally made the call. Sat in my car in the parking lot with the card in my hand.

"Yeah, I'm trying to get in with one of your counselors," I said when somebody picked up. "I don't remember her name, she was real good though. Worked with me and my wife about two years ago."

"Do you have a date of service or any other information?" the secretary asked.

"Nah, not on me. But she was real good. Helped us a lot."

I heard typing. "Can you describe her at all?"

I thought about it. "Older lady. Real calm. Didn't take no shit either."

More typing. A pause. "That sounds like it might be Ms. Aliza Ishmael."

"Yeah," I said.

"Unfortunately, Ms. Ishmael is no longer a counselor here." She said it gentle, like she knew that wasn't what I wanted to hear. "But if you're looking for someone with a similar approach, we have Ms. Britnie Holloway. She's been getting really great feedback from her clients. Very down to earth, very direct. Would you like me to set up an initial consultation?"

"Yeah," I said. "I guess so."

"Great. She has a Thursday opening at six PM, or a Saturday morning at ten."

"Saturday," I said. Easier to get to without rearranging work.

"Perfect. Can I get your name and a callback number?"

I gave her everything she needed and hung up. Sat there for a minute looking out the windshield at the parking lot. I didn't know what I was expecting to feel after making that call. Relief, maybe. I just felt tired.

I went back inside and tried to focus on the rest of my shift.

***

It wasn't working.

I had been at the plant for six hours and genuinely checked out for five of them. I was running pallets down the line when I almost stacked a full load wrong, weight distribution off, the whole thing shifting before I caught it, my spotter yelling from across the floor. I got it steady but my heart was beating fast as fuck. That was the kind of mistake that put people on the ground. I got my head right for the last hour, but it shook me.

I clocked out and went straight home.

***

The new house still felt new in the way that empty walls and boxes you hadn't finished unpacking felt new. But it was mine. No history in it. No argument that had happened in that kitchen, no silence that had sat too long in that hallway. Just clean space that I was slowly making into something.

Saviour had already picked his room, the bigger one, like I promised, second biggest to mine. He had been over twice since the move and both times he acted new about it, running through the rooms, claiming territory, asking about the TV I had told him we would talk about and then gone ahead and put in anyway. That part felt right. Building something for him to come home to.

I was almost sleep when my phone buzzed.

Sena: *Just wanted to check on you.*

I stared at the screen. Read it twice. Set the phone down. Picked it back up.

I started typing: *Fuck you.*

Sat there looking at it. Then deleted it.

The damage was done.

I left it on read and turned on *Do Not Disturb*.

Chapter 11

3 Weeks Later
Kia

We were at the gate at *Hartsfield-Jackson* at 6 AM, and I had already decided that Tool was never allowed to book a morning flight again.

Saviour had been up since 4:30 on pure adrenaline. I had been up since 4:30 because of Saviour. Tool somehow looked completely rested and unbothered, standing at the *Delta* counter with carry-ons for three like it was noon.

"You're too awake for this hour," I told him.

"I'm excited," he said.

Everybody had flown in separately. Tia and Nard and the kids out of the same terminal; Toot right behind them. Ms. Kristen and Mr. Robert had done a direct with *Southwest*, and Tamia had called me twice from security because Semaj had a juice box in his backpack that held up the whole line.

"I told him to drink it before we left," she said when she finally made it to the gate looking like she already had a full day.

"Brielle okay?" I asked.

"Brielle is perfect. Semaj is on his last warning," she said, pulling him along.

Saviour ran straight to Nala and they picked up wherever they left off like no time had passed. BJ gave Saviour a dap, and just like that, the kids had their own little group and the adults had forty seconds of peace.

***

Tool had handled the shirts.

He had coordinated with everybody ahead of time and had them packed and distributed at the *Airbnb* the first night. Each family had their own set.

Tool, me, and Saviour were Mickey, Minnie, and baby Mickey.

Tia, Nard, Nala, and BJ were *Toy Story*: Tia in Jessie, Nard in Woody, Nala as Bo Peep, and BJ, who had tried to negotiate his way out of it until he saw that his shirt said Buzz Lightyear and then suddenly had no complaints.

Toot had Lilo.

Ms. Kristen and Mr. Robert had classic Mickey and Minnie. Mr. Robert had put his on without a word, wearing it with the quiet dignity of a man who didn't need to talk to be heard. But Ms. Kristen took her time, looking at hers, measuring the moment. She then locked eyes with Tool in a way that made everything else in the *Airbnb* go quiet.

"You did good, baby," she said. She didn't have to scream it; that smooth, measured way she talked made it hit harder than an excited shout anyway. In her world, "good" was a high bar, and Tool had just cleared it with room to spare.

Tamia had her squad in *Encanto* gear. She was Mirabel, while Brielle was Isabela, looking perfect and knowing it. Semaj was Camilo, which was a read in itself. Tamia swore it was nail on the head because that boy stayed doing the absolute most, shapeshifting his attitude every fifteen minutes just to see what he could get away with.

We all walked into *Magic Kingdom* on day one looking coordinated, and I watched strangers stop and smile at us as we passed.

***

Day one was *Magic Kingdom* and we did all of it. Saviour and Nala rode the *Tomorrowland Speedway* three times back-to-back and refused to come off. BJ and Semaj ended up somewhere around *Space Mountain* and became inseparable for the rest of the trip. Brielle attached herself to Tia, who was the kind of woman who made every kid in her vicinity feel included, and Tamia floated between conversations like she had known these people for years.

She pulled me aside around lunchtime.

"Kia," she said.

"I know," I said.

"I like them."

"I know, Tamia."

"Like genuinely. Ms. Kristen hugged me when she met me," she said. "She didn't have to do that."

"That's just how they are," I said.

She pointed her corn dog at me. "You better not fuck this up."

"Nobody's fuckin' anything up," I said, and she gave me a look.

***

Day two was *EPCOT*. The adults did the most eating and the least walking. Tool and Nard found a beer garden situation in the *Germany Pavilion* and were there for a minute. Me and Tool's mama walked the *World Showcase* together while Mr. Robert sat somewhere with Tank on *FaceTime*. She asked me about my job, about how I ended up in my field, about Saviour and what he was like. I was talking more than I planned to.

Tamia caught up with us and slid right in like she been there the whole time.

"Ms. Kristen, do you have any single brothers?" she asked.

"Tamia," I said.

"What? I'm asking for myself."

Ms. Kristen laughed, surprised. "I have two. One is too old for you and one is too much trouble."

"I'll take the trouble one," Tamia said.

Ms. Kristen looked at me. "I like her."

"Everybody likes her," I said. "That's the problem."

***

Sometime on day two, late afternoon, while we were waiting for the kids to finish a ride . . .

I was standing with Tool and Toot and I stepped away to take a call from Tamia that got lost somewhere near the *Japan Pavilion.* When I came back, I was mid-sentence telling Tool about Sacavè having called earlier about Saviour.

"Saviour wasn't answering his *iPad*, but I told him he's been with the kids all day, he's fine, I'll have him call when we get back to the room—"

I noticed Toot go still. Just slightly. The way somebody does when something clicks but they're not ready to say it out loud yet. She was looking down at her phone, but she wasn't looking at her phone.

I kept talking and she kept not saying anything.

***

Sacavè had called twice while we were in the park. I caught the second one and stepped to the side.

"He's not answering," Sacavè said when I picked up. No hello.

"He's been on rides all day with the other kids. His *iPad* is in the room," I said.

"I'm just saying, he should be accessible—"

"Sacavè, he's five. He's at *Disney World*. He is accessible through me. I'll have him call you tonight," I said.

A pause. "A'ight."

That was the whole conversation.

That night, I handed Saviour the *iPad* before bath time and listened from the bathroom as he told Sacavè about every single ride in detail, sometimes going back to correct himself, sometimes asking me to confirm the name of something. By the end of it, Sacavè was laughing on the other end. I heard it through the door. Whatever he felt about the circumstances, he showed up for that call and Saviour didn't feel any of the rest of it.

I was grateful for that, even when I didn't say so.

***

Day three was *Hollywood Studios* and the kids ran that park. *Tower of Terror* had Semaj and BJ looking less confident coming off than they had going on. Saviour was too short to ride it and had a full attitude about it for ten minutes before Nala dragged him off to something else.

We stood in line for *Slinky Dog Dash.*

Tool was talking to his dad ahead of us, laughing about something, and Saviour was watching them.

"Pops," Tool said, getting his father's attention about something.

Saviour looked up at me. Then back at Tool. Then—

"Pops," he called out, tugging Tool's shirt.

Tool looked down, but before he fully broke away from the conversation with his father, he locked eyes with him, then gave a sharp, subtle nod and a quick index finger pointed toward Saviour, the universal man-code for *hold that thought, the little man needs me first*. Mr. Robert didn't say a word. He just had a knowing, heavy-lidded smile across his face as he watched his son step into the same shoes he had been wearing for over three decades.

"Yeah?" Tool asked, leaning down.

Saviour pointed at the ride. "Can I sit in the front?"

"We'll see when we get up there," Tool said, and they kept moving.

I stood there for a second.

Tool hadn't reacted to the name. Hadn't made a thing of it, hadn't looked back at me, hadn't done anything except answer like it was completely natural. And Saviour had moved on like it was natural too.

It felt warm and complicated at the same time, and I got in the cart when it was our turn and didn't say anything about it yet.

***

That night after the kids were down, I told Tool.

We were on the back porch of the *Airbnb* with the little string lights on and everybody else inside, and I said, "Saviour called you Pops today."

Tool nodded. "I heard."

"You didn't say anything."

"What was I supposed to say?"

I looked at him. "I don't know. Something."

"He heard me call my dad Pops and he went with it," Tool said. "I wasn't gone make him feel weird about it."

"Does it—" I started. "Are you okay with that?"

He looked at me for a minute. "Kia. I love that boy."

I nodded and looked out at the yard. He reached over and covered my hand with his and we sat there until the conversation moved to something else, but I held onto that for the rest of the night.

***

Day four was *Animal Kingdom*.

The morning was easy, safaris and trails and Saviour spending forty minutes convinced he was going to personally spot a lion. Toot walked with me for most of the morning while the guys did their thing with the kids, and she was easy to be around in a way that felt familiar. We talked about her marriage vaguely. I didn't push. We just walked and talked and let it be what it was.

That afternoon, Tool said he wanted to take me somewhere. Just us for an hour. Ms. Kristen took Saviour without me even having to ask.

We walked to a garden area. The noise dropped down to almost nothing. I thought maybe he just wanted a minute alone, and I was fine with that.

Then he turned to face me and reached into the pocket of his shorts.

"Tool—"

"Let me talk," he said.

I closed my mouth.

"I knew from the first time I saw you." He said it the same way he had in *Destin*. "I told you that. I'm not saying it again to be romantic; I'm saying it because I want you to understand that everything I've done since then has been on purpose. I don't do things I'm not sure about." He opened the box. The ring caught the light. "You're officially single. I love you. I love your son. I want to build with you for real." He looked at me. "Kia Williams. Will you marry me?"

I looked at the ring. Then at him. Then at the ring again.

There was a part of me that wanted to say everything I had said before: *I'm not sure I want to get married again, I need more time, I'm still figuring out who I am outside of being somebody's wife.* All of it was still true. All of it was still sitting in me somewhere.

But he was looking at me with so much certainty.

"Yes," I said.

He slid the ring on my finger and stood up and pulled me in, and I let him hold me and tried to sort through what I was feeling while his arms were around me. Joy was in there. Real joy. Love was in there. And underneath all of it, something that felt less like a yes and more like I hadn't wanted to be the reason that look left his face.

I pushed it down.

***

When we got back to the group, it took approximately four seconds for Nala to spot the ring.

After that, it was noise. Good noise, Tia screaming, Tamia grabbing my hand and staring at the ring like she was appraising it, Mr. Robert shaking Tool's hand with both of his, Saviour asking what happened and then being told and not fully understanding but clapping anyway because everybody else was.

Ms. Kristen hugged Tool first. Then she came to me.

Her hug was warmer than the air kisses at dinner.

"Congratulations, baby," she said.

"Thank you, Ms. Kristen."

She pulled back and looked at me. The same way she had looked at Tool when she thought nobody was watching during dinner at his house that first night.

"Come walk with me for a minute," she said.

***

We found a bench near the garden entrance. She sat with the posture she always had, hands folded, and for a moment she just looked out at the path in front of us.

"I saw your face," she said.

I didn't pretend not to know what she meant. "Ms. Kristen—"

"I'm not saying it to start anything. I'm saying it because I love my son, and I love what I see when he looks at you." She turned to me. "And I want to make sure you're in this the same way he is."

I looked down at the ring. "I love him."

"I know you do. That part I can see too," she said. "My son has wanted a family of his own for a long time. Longer than you probably know. He doesn't say it the way some men do; he just moves toward it. Everything he does is pointed in that direction." She looked at me. "I just want to know that you want the same things."

"I'm scared," I said, and I didn't plan to say it but it came out before I could think about it. "I was married before, and I know how that ends, and I—" I stopped. "I love him. I do. I just don't want to bring that fear into something that deserves better than it."

She nodded slow. "That's honest."

"I'm trying to be."

She reached over and covered my hand with hers, the one with the ring on it. "Fear and love can live in the same place," she said. "The question is which one you let drive." She squeezed once and stood up. "You're good for him. I see that. I just needed to see that you knew it too."

She walked back toward the group and I sat there for a minute.

Then I got up and went back to my family.

Chapter 12

1 Year Later

I never thought this day would come.

I swore I would never say "I do" again. Never let another man have that kind of hold on me. But here I am, thirty minutes away from becoming Mrs. Kia Warren.

My bridesmaids are Myra, Tamia, Ness, my soon-to-be sister-in-law Tia, and my childhood best friend Victoria. My flower girls are Nala and Brielle, and my ring bearer, of course, is my handsome son, Saviour.

And yes, my man is wearing pink.

A soft pink, but pink nonetheless. He agreed without hesitation, the same way he did with everything since the day we met almost two years ago. I didn't have to convince him on the color either. It symbolized peace, forgiveness, and a fresh start, everything this love stands for. The way he loves me is what every woman deserves: steady, intentional, and real.

I fought almost a year for my divorce from Sacavè, and in the end, it was poetic justice that his "best friend" forged his signature on those papers. She thought she was playing me, but really, she freed me. She did me and my husband-to-be a favor.

Standing in the bridal suite, I could hear the faint melody of the string quartet warming up outside. My hands were shaky as I smoothed down the front of my dress, a beautiful ivory mermaid gown with lace appliqués going down the train. The bodice hugged me perfectly.

"Girl, you better stop touching that dress before you mess it up," Myra said, swatting my hand away. She looked gorgeous in her soft pink bridesmaid dress; the color complemented her deep brown skin.

"I'm just nervous," I admitted.

"Nervous? Girl, that man out there is probably losing his mind waiting for you," Tamia chimed in, adjusting her own dress in the mirror.

Victoria handed me a glass of champagne. "Here. Sip."

I took the glass but didn't drink. I stared at my reflection in the full-length mirror. My makeup was flawless: soft glam, smokey eye, and a nude lip. My hair was pulled back into a low bun with a few curls that Myra had touched up twice because I kept running my fingers through them.

Tia came up beside me in the mirror, her pink dress fitted and pretty, and bumped my shoulder with hers. She didn't say anything. She didn't need to. She became one of my people in the space of a year in that quiet way that real ones do. No announcement, no production, just consistent presence until one day you realize you can't imagine not having her around. Having her standing beside me today felt right in a way I hadn't expected it to until now.

"Mommy, you look beautiful." Saviour burst through the door, his tuxedo perfectly tailored, pink bow tie matching the groomsmen, pillow already in his hands like he was already given the rundown and was taking his assignment seriously. My heart swelled looking at him.

"Thank you, baby," I said, kneeling down to hug him. "You look so handsome. Are you ready to walk down that aisle?"

"Yes." He held the pillow up proudly.

There was a soft knock and my Uncle Mario poked his head in. "It's time, baby girl."

"Gotta go," Saviour said, and was back out the door before I could say anything else.

I laughed. Stood up. Took one last look in the mirror.

Myra straightened my train. Tamia handed me my bouquet, blush and ivory roses, exactly what I had asked for.

***

Oh, I prayed for you / Oh, I cried for you / I can't believe we're here at last . . .

I walked down the aisle to Teeks' "First Time," and although it wasn't my first time getting married, it was my first time walking toward my husband-to-be with certainty and peace. Arm in arm with my Uncle Mario, every step felt sacred. I looked around and admired every detail: the blush and ivory florals cascading from tall gold centerpieces, the sheer draping that made an ethereal canopy above us, the soft candlelight flickering along the aisle. Everything was exactly what I had imagined and more.

Can you take me through? / Oh Touch me on my face / Kiss me on my hand / Take me to a place where we find love . . .

Tool was already falling apart with a hand over his mouth, his best man, Enrique, already positioned with tissues like he had been expecting this. My big, steady, unshakeable man was standing at that altar completely undone, and it took everything in me not to pick up this dress and run to him.

Show me what it means / And how it's supposed to feel

"Ma, why are you crying?" Saviour asked loudly from beside Tool, looking up at him with genuine concern.

The entire venue laughed. Tool, still crying, reached over and gently dabbed my face with a tissue before I even realized my own tears had started falling.

"Happy tears, baby," I managed.

"I know that's right," Myra yelled from behind me.

Snaps. More laughter. The officiant chuckled at his own podium.

"Amen . . . Amen," he said, getting himself together.

My uncle placed my hand in Tool's. He looked at me like I was everything he had been working toward. I looked back at him the same way.

***

The officiant, Pastor Derrick, who had known Tool's family for years, opened with a prayer that settled the whole room. He spoke about covenant, about choosing, about the difference between love as a feeling and love as a decision made every morning. He talked about second chances not as consolation prizes but as God's precision, the idea that sometimes the first road has to close before the right one opens.

I felt that in my bones.

When he asked if anyone had cause to object to the union, the room went church-quiet for exactly one second.

Then Tool's groomsmen, all five of them, reached into their jackets simultaneously.

The glint of metal caught the light before I fully processed what was happening, and then the laughter started because every single one of them had come prepared. A few guests in the front rows leaned back instinctively before realizing what was going on. Tamia screamed from the bridesmaid line. Myra covered her mouth with her bouquet.

"Nobody objecting to nothing today," Enrique announced calmly, still holding his piece like he was ready to negotiate.

Tool hadn't even flinched. Just stood there looking at me with that smirk.

"Put them up," Pastor Derrick said, shaking his head with a smile that said he had been warned this might happen. "Lord have mercy. Let's continue."

The room was still laughing when we turned back to each other. Tool squeezed my hands and I squeezed back, and somehow, I loved him even more for the fact that this was the energy he had brought into the most important moment of our lives.

***

When it was time for vows, Tool took both of my hands.

"Kia," he began, his voice thick with emotion, "I don't believe in coincidences. I believe God placed you at that *QuikTrip* on that random Tuesday because He knew we both needed each other. You walked into my life with your guard up, your walls high, and your heart guarded, and I don't blame you. But you gave me a chance. You let me prove that love doesn't have to hurt, that it can heal, and that it can be safe."

He paused, wiped his eyes.

"I vow to protect your peace, to honor your heart, and to show you every single day that you made the right choice. Saviour, my son," he looked down at Saviour standing there with his pillow, wide-eyed and still. "I vow to love you, guide you, and be the example of a man you deserve. You two are my everything, and I will spend the rest of my life making sure you both know it."

I was gone. The tears flowed and I stopped caring about the makeup.

When it was my turn, I took a deep breath.

"Tevin, you taught me that love isn't loud. It's quiet. It's consistent. It's showing up even when it's hard. You loved me through my healing, through my mess, through my doubt. You never rushed me, never pressured me, and never made me feel like I wasn't enough. You are everything I prayed for and more. I vow to love you, to support you, and to build a life with you that honors God and the love He gave us. Thank you for choosing me. Thank you for choosing us."

Nala was crying in the flower girl line. She was seven years old and she was genuinely crying, and I almost lost it completely looking at her.

We exchanged rings.

"By the power vested in me," the pastor said, "I now pronounce you husband and wife." He smiled wide. "You may salute your bride."

Tool held my face, leaned in, and kissed me like the room wasn't full of people.

The crowd clapped. Myra was the loudest thing in the building. Tamia was right behind her. I could hear Saviour somewhere in the noise going "ewwww" and I laughed against Tool's lips and he laughed back, and Pastor Derrick was saying something but neither of us heard it for another few seconds.

"Ladies and gentlemen," Pastor Derrick finally announced over the noise, arms raised, "Mr. and Mrs. Tevin Warren."

***

Photos took the better part of an hour. The photographer moved us through the venue with altar shots, garden shots, bridal party, family. Saviour was cooperative for all of twelve minutes before he realized that BJ and Semaj were somewhere on the property, and then we had to negotiate to keep him in frame.

Tool's parents. My mother. The whole bridal party together on the steps was picture perfect. Me and Tia and Tamia and Myra with our heads together laughing at something Tamia said that I can't even repeat here. Tool and his groomsmen looking like they had been put together by someone who knew exactly what they were doing.

And then just us. Me and Tool in the garden, the photographer backing up to give us space, and him pulling me in by the small of my back the way he always did and looking at me the way he always did, and I forgot there was a camera at all.

***

Introducing Mr. and Mrs. Tevin Warren.

The reception hall doors opened and the DJ set it off. We walked in to everybody clapping, money raining down like we was in *Blue Flames*. I was laughing and trying to block my face and Tool had his arm up like he was accepting an award, and the energy in that room was everything I will never forget for the rest of my life.

Dinner was served, everything good. Toasts came after. Enrique went first and had the room in tears and then laughing inside of three minutes, the mark of someone who actually knew how to give a toast. Tamia stood up without being asked, which was on brand, and said embarrassing shit. Tia kept hers short and sweet.

Ms. Kristen stood last.

The room quieted differently for her. She didn't use notes. She stood with her champagne glass and looked at her son first, then at me, and said, "I always knew the woman who was meant for my son would be the kind of woman who could receive everything he had to give without flinching. Kia, I see you receive him. I see you receive all of it. And that is the greatest gift you could have given this family." She raised her glass. "Welcome home, baby."

There was not a dry eye at the head table.

We cut the cake, chocolate on the inside, Tool's request; ivory fondant on the outside. He smiled the whole time he was feeding me my slice like he was proud of himself for his restraint.

***

Then our first dance.

And as you cried in my arms / You woke up my heart / And I saw again what I found in you 'Cause her heart, her heart won't let me lose her / No matter how I try I just can't say goodbye and lose her . . .

Tool had picked this song and sung it to me so many times over the past year that I knew every word. Hearing it in that room, with his arms around my waist and my head on his chest, I fell in love with it all over again. He swayed us slow, just holding me.

After our dance, I went to Saviour.

Queen Naija's "Mama's Hand" started and my son, my ring bearer, my reason, my whole heart in a tiny tuxedo, took my hand seriously and walked me to the floor like he had been practicing. He had been practicing.

We danced and he was focused and at some point he looked up at me and said, "Mommy, are you happy?"

"So happy, baby," I said.

"Good," he said, and went back to counting his steps.

Across the floor Tool was dancing with Ms. Kristen, her head against his chest the way mine had just been against his, and he was holding her the way a son holds his mother when he understands what she sacrificed. She was crying. He wasn't trying to stop her. I watched them over Saviour's head and felt something so full.

***

The bouquet toss brought out a competitive energy from the single women in the room. Tamia had positioned herself in the back like she was running a play, and when the bouquet went up, she came through the crowd and caught it clean, held it up.

Then the DJ slowed things down to something low and suggestive, and Tool appeared in front of me with a look on his face that told me exactly what was coming next.

Ro James came through the speakers with "Permission," and Tool pulled me to the middle of the floor and took his time getting down to the garter. The groomsmen yelled all kind of shit while he was doing it. Tool was completely unbothered by all of it, moving at his own pace, looking up at me with that smirk at every reaction he pulled from the crowd. By the time he stood back up, the room was in rare form and I was somewhere between embarrassed and deeply in love with him.

He launched the garter into the groomsmen and Enrique took a running dive for it that the DJ gave a sound effect to.

***

Then the room quieted for something different.

The foot-washing had been my idea. Tool had agreed to it the same way he agreed to most things I brought to him with intention. We sat across from each other in the center of the reception floor with a basin between us.

I washed his feet first. The room was still enough that I could hear the water. I thought about everything it meant: service, humility, choosing someone not just in the good moments but in the ordinary ones. He kept his eyes on me the entire time.

Then he knelt in front of me.

Seeing a man like Tool, solid, unshakeable, and respected, kneel in front of me in a room full of everyone who loved us was a statement that didn't need a single word. He took my foot in his hands like it was the most fragile thing he'd ever held, bringing that same protective gentleness that made me feel safe even in the dark. My heart did a slow, heavy roll in my chest. I put my hand over my mouth, the weight of his devotion pressing against my spirit until I could do nothing but leak tears. Tia made a sound behind me. Somewhere in the room, I heard Ms. Kristen.

He looked up at me when he finished. Didn't say anything. Didn't need to.

I reached down and pulled him up and he kissed me in front of everybody again, and the room came back to life around us.

***

Later that night, as we climbed into the car headed to the airport, I turned to Tool, panicking.

"Baby, you have your passport, right?" I asked.

We were headed on our fourth trip together, this time, our red-eye flight to *Paris* for our honeymoon. Our first trip had been *San Juan*. Our second, *Destin*, where he asked me to be his girlfriend. Our third, *Disney World* with the family, where he asked me to be his wife. Now here we were, headed out of the country to the most romantic place in the world. Ya girl had been using up that PTO like crazy.

"Yeah, it's in your purse, bae," Tool answered, calm.

"My purse?" I checked. I did not remember putting his passport in my purse.

"I dropped it in there when your purse was sitting on the island," he said, rubbing my back.

We looked at each other and I laughed. He already knew my anxiety was about to get the best of me and had handled it before I even got there. That was him. Always three steps ahead, always with a solution, never making me feel like my worry was an inconvenience.

Sacavè had declined the wedding invitation and then turned around and refused to keep Saviour during the honeymoon too, which had told me everything I needed to know about where his head still was. I cried a little on the way to the airport, ten days was the longest I had ever been away from my baby. But Saviour's presence was in such high demand that it worked itself out between my mother,

Tool's parents, and Tia. He was going to be fine. Better than fine.

We were also in the middle of building our home. The land had been Saviour's and my Christmas gift from Tool. We decided to rent out both of our current houses once the build was done. I wanted us in something that had only ever been ours. No one either of us had been with had ever walked those floors or slept in those rooms. Tool had only two requests: a pool and a theater/game room. Everything else he handed to me.

As the plane lifted off, I looked over at him. Already asleep, hand resting on my thigh, like even unconscious, he knew where he wanted to be.

I smiled. Closed my eyes.

I couldn't wait to make love to my husband in another country.

Chapter 13

The flight to Paris was long, damn near nine hours, but it was well worth it when we finally touched down. The city is everything I imagined and more. Beautiful architecture everywhere you look, people dressed like they stepped out of a magazine, and that romantic Parisian vibe in the air. Even the way they spoke French sounded elegant.

"Baby, this is beautiful," I said as we walked into our hotel room at the *Hôtel Plaza Athénée*.

Neither of us had been to Paris before, so we had to rely heavy on reviews and recommendations from people who had been. This hotel had the most five-star reviews, and I could definitely see why. Our suite was so pretty: windows overlooking the *Eiffel Tower*, a king-sized bed with the softest sheets I had ever felt, a marble bathroom with a soaking tub big enough for two, and a sitting area with a bottle of champagne waiting for us on ice.

"This is nice, bae," Tool said, walking over to the window and looking out at the view. "We're really in Paris right now."

"We are," I said, coming up behind him and wrapping my arms around his waist. "Mr. and Mrs. Warren in Paris for our honeymoon. This don't even feel real."

He turned around and kissed me. "It's real. And we 'bout to enjoy every second of it."

To celebrate our love and marriage in the City of Love felt so intentional, so right. I couldn't wait to explore the city with my husband, the *Eiffel Tower*, the *Louvre*, the cafés, all of it. But for now, we needed sleep. The time difference was six hours ahead of *Atlanta*, and we were both exhausted from the flight and the wedding.

"Let's take a nap, then we can go see the vibes," Tool suggested, already pulling off his shoes.

"Okay," I agreed, climbing into the bed.

We knocked out within minutes, wrapped up in each other, jet-lagged but happy.

***

When I woke up a few hours later, it was early evening in *Paris*. The sun was starting to set. Tool was still sleeping next to me, snoring. I grabbed my phone to check the time and saw I had a missed *FaceTime* call from my mama.

I called her back.

She answered on the second ring. "Hey, baby girl. How's Paris?"

"It's beautiful, Mama. I just woke up from a nap. How's my baby doing?" I asked.

"He's good. Playing his game right now. Hold on, let me get him," she said.

A few seconds later, Saviour's face popped up on the screen, and my heart melted.

"Hey, Ma," he said, all smiles.

"Hey, baby. I miss you so much. Are you being good for Suga?" I asked.

"Yes. Look what she got me," he said, holding up a new game.

"That's so cool, papa," I said.

Then his face got serious. "Ma, where's Dad?"

My stomach dropped. Saviour had started calling Tool "Pops" a few months ago, so I knew he wasn't asking about him. He was asking about Sacavè.

That question frustrated the hell out of me because it was one I didn't have an answer to. We had been in Paris for less than a day, but according to my mama, Sacavè hadn't called or *FaceTimed* Saviour. Not once.

"Did you try calling him, baby?" I asked.

"I tried everything, Ma. I called and texted and he didn't answer," Saviour said.

I wanted to cuss Sacavè out. Right then and there.

"Baby, I'm sure Daddy is just busy working. You know how he gets sometimes," I lied, trying to make my son feel better even though I was pissed.

"Okay," Saviour said, but I could tell he didn't believe me.

"I love you so much, Saviour. You know that, right? And Pops loves you too. We'll be home soon, okay?" I said.

"Okay. Love you, Ma. Tell Pops I said what's up," he said.

"I will, baby. Be good."

We hung up, and I just sat there staring at my phone, feeling myself get more and more pissed. Tool moved, then turned toward me, noticing something was wrong.

"What's up, baby? You good?" he asked, sitting up.

"No. Saviour just asked about Sacavè. Said he's been trying to call him and he won't answer," I said.

Tool's jaw clenched. "He ignoring him?"

"Apparently. And you know why. He's in his feelings about the wedding. So now he taking it out on Saviour," I said.

"That's some sucka shit," Tool said, shaking his head.

"I know. When shit don't go his way, he shut down and everybody around him gotta suffer," I said.

I knew this pattern. When things got hard or when he felt like he wasn't in control, Sacavè would withdraw, go silent, ignore calls, disappear into his own world. But he had never done it to Saviour. Not like this.

"You want me to call him?" Tool offered.

"No. That's not gonna make it nothing but worse," I said.

Tool pulled me into his arms. "A'ight."

***

We tried to shake off the mood and got ready to head out for the evening. I put on a fitted black wrap dress, gold jewelry, and some heels that had no business being that comfortable. Tool threw on some jeans, a tee, and his *Jordans*. We looked good together.

Our first stop was dinner at this restaurant called *Le Cinq* that our concierge recommended. It was fancy, like *Michelin*-star fancy. The kind of place where you need a reservation months in advance, but somehow Tool had worked his magic and got us in.

"How you even get us a reservation here?" I asked as we walked in.

"Don't worry about it," he said with a smirk, making the money hand signal.

The food was so good. I couldn't pronounce half the shit on the menu, so I just pointed and hoped for the best. But everything that came out was like art on a plate: beautiful and delicious.

"This is the fanciest meal I ever had in my life," I admitted, cutting into my perfectly cooked steak.

"To the first of everything," Tool said, raising his glass of wine.

We toasted.

After dinner, we walked along the *Seine River*, holding hands. The *Eiffel Tower* was lit up in the distance, sparkling like something out of a movie.

"We gotta go up there tomorrow," I said, pointing at the tower.

"Whatever you want, baby. This your trip. I'm just here to make sure you happy," Tool said.

"I am happy. You make me happy," I said, standing on my tiptoes to kiss him.

Everything about Paris felt romantic and perfect.

But in the back of my mind, I couldn't stop thinking about my son and how his father was letting him down.

***

When we got back to the hotel, I decided to call Sacavè. It was late in Paris but early evening in *Atlanta*, so I knew he would be up.

The phone rang. And rang. And rang. Then went to voicemail.

I tried again. Same thing, pacing back and forth.

"This nigga ignoring me too," I said, frustrated.

"Let it go for tonight, bae. We'll deal with it tomorrow," Tool said.

But I couldn't let it go. I sent Sacavè a text: *You need to call your son. He's been trying to reach you and thinks you're ignoring him. Whatever you got going on with me, don't take it out on Saviour. He don't deserve that.*

I stared at my phone, waiting for the three dots to pop up showing he was typing. But they never did. It hadn't even said delivered.

"Come here," Tool said, opening his arms.

I put my phone down and climbed into bed. He held me, rubbing my back, trying to calm me down.

"I just don't understand how he could do this," I said.

"Because he's hurt. And hurt people hurt people. But that don't make it right," Tool said.

"It don't. And Saviour is the one suffering because of it," I said.

"I know, baby. But Saviour got us. He got you, he got me, he got your mama, my mama. He's surrounded by love. Sacavè's the one missing out," Tool said.

He was right. But it still hurt knowing my son was wondering why his daddy wasn't answering his calls.

I wasn't in the mood for sex with all this going on, even after all I talked about was slutting my husband out in Paris.

***

The next morning, we woke up early to hit up the *Eiffel Tower* before the crowds got too crazy. We got tickets to go all the way to the top, and the view was everything. You could see the entire city from up there.

“This is *nice*,” I said, looking out over *Paris*.

We took a million selfies.

After the *Eiffel Tower*, we went to the *Louvre*. I’m not really a museum person, but it was nice. We saw the *Mona Lisa*, which was smaller than I expected. We walked around for hours, looking at all the art and sculptures.

“I feel cultured as hell right now,” Tool joked.

“Right? Like we’re sophisticated and shit,” I said, laughing.

We got lunch at a little café near the museum, then walked around the streets of *Paris*, going into shops and boutiques. I bought Saviour a few souvenirs: a little *Eiffel Tower* keychain and some chocolates.

Somewhere between the third boutique and the fourth glass of wine at a little sidewalk bar Tool saw tucked between two shops, we went from sightseeing to full-on tipsy. The wine here was different, smoother, lighter, but it creeped up on you. By the time we stumbled back onto the street laughing at nothing, I knew we were done for the day.

“We need to go back to the room,” I said, grabbing Tool’s arm to steady myself in my heels.

“That’s what I been saying,” he said, already waving down a car.

***

Back at the hotel, the energy shifted the second the door closed behind us. The alcohol had loosened everything. I sat on the edge of the bed and watched Tool move around the room, and something about the way he looked just did something to me.

I thought about how much I had been in mama mode since Saviour was born. How even after I fell in love with Tool, I was always mama first, everything else second. Making sure Saviour was good, making sure pickups happened, making sure homework got done, making sure somebody wasn't hurting my kid's feelings from across the ocean. I had been so focused on being his mother that I hadn't even fully stepped into being this man's wife yet.

And we were in Paris. On our honeymoon.

I stood up, walked over to Tool, and put my hands on his chest.

"I owe you," I said.

He looked down at me, reading my face. "Owe me what?"

"I been so caught up in everything with Saviour that I ain't been giving you what you deserve. We in Paris, baby. On our honeymoon. I been acting like we just roommates taking a trip," I said.

"You good, Kia. You a mama first—"

"I'm your wife first tonight," I said, cutting him off.

I reached up and kissed him. His hands found my waist and pulled me against him like he'd been waiting. I could feel how much he wanted me, and knowing that lit something up inside me.

We moved to the bed. When things slowed down enough for him to reach for the nightstand, I stopped him.

"Don't," I said.

He paused. "Don't what?"

"Don't get one. I want to feel you," I said.

He looked at me for a second, and a smile spread across his face.

"Shit, you ain't even gotta tell me twice," he said. "Didn't wanna use one anyway. I'm not tryna keep fucking my wife with a condom. I need to feel what's mine."

And after that, there was no more talking.

What happened in that hotel room in Paris, in that king-sized bed with the *Eiffel Tower* visible through the window, was between me and my husband. All I'll say is that the soaking tub got used, the champagne that had been sitting on ice since we checked in finally got opened, and by the time it was over, I understood why people said Paris changed you.

We passed out after, wrapped up in each other, the city glowing outside our window.

***

That evening, we got dressed up for a fancy dinner cruise on the *Seine*. It was so romantic: soft music playing, delicious food, the city lights reflecting off the water.

"This trip has been everything," I said, sipping my wine.

"It really has. I'm glad we doing this," Tool said.

"Me too. I love you so much," I said.

"I love you too, Mrs. Warren," he said, and hearing my new last name made me smile so hard.

When we got back to the hotel, I *FaceTimed* Saviour before he went to bed.

"Hi, Ma. Hi, Pops," Saviour said when he answered.

"Hey, man. We miss you," Tool said, waving at the camera.

"I miss you too. Did you buy me something?" Saviour asked.

"You know I did. I got you all kinds of stuff," I said.

"Okay. Did Daddy call you?" he asked, and my heart sank.

"Not yet, baby. But I'm sure he will soon," I lied again.

"Okay," Saviour said, but I could see the disappointment written all over his face.

We talked for a few more minutes about his day, what he ate, what games he played, what movie he watched with Suga. Then we said goodnight and *I love yous*. After we hung up, I just sat there staring at my phone.

Still no response from Sacavè. Not to my texts. Not to my calls. Nothing.

"I'm calling him again," I said, my frustration building.

I dialed his number. It rang once, then went straight to voicemail like he hit decline.

"This motherfucka," I said, calling right back.

Same thing. Straight to voicemail.

"He's really ignoring me. He's really out here ignoring his son and now ignoring me when I'm trying to talk to him about ignoring his son," I said, my voice getting louder with each word.

Tool sat up in the bed. "Call off the room phone."

"Right. Because clearly he don't wanna hear shit I got to say," I said, handing Tool my phone with Sacavè's number pulled up.

"I got you, baby," Tool said, taking the phone.

I watched as he dialed, putting it on speaker so I could hear. My heart was pounding.

The phone rang. And rang.

"He probably won't answer for this number either," I said.

But then, just before it was about to go to voicemail, someone picked up.

"Man, hello," Sacavè's voice came through, sounding irritated.

And just like that, I snapped.

"Sacavè, why the fuck are you ignoring my son?" I yelled into the phone before Tool could even say anything.

Chapter 14

Sacavè

I don't never sleep at night. I just lay in the dark. And in the daytime, I have nightmares of you breaking my heart . . .

Rod Wave sing like he lived every bit of pain I been going through. Watching my life fall apart in real time. This song is exactly how I feel right now, stuck in my feelings, replaying memories I should probably let go of but can't. Counseling ain't doing shit these days. Britnie's fine ass sitting there asking me questions I don't got answers to, and I'm paying her $150 an hour for the privilege. I spend more time wondering what she looks like outside of those tight-ass pencil skirts more than I do working on my "inner peace". The music was more therapeutic these days. Them hour-long sessions were where I just end up more frustrated.

I crashed out so bad two days ago. Sena wouldn't stop blowing up my phone, back-to-back calls, text after text, whole paragraphs about how she just wanted to talk, how she needed me to understand where she was coming from. I really thought she would let it go. The damage was done. I got so fed up with seeing her name pop up on my screen that I threw my phone straight through the goddamn wall. The whole screen shattered. Couldn't see shit on that bitch.

Now that I think about it, I probably could've just put it on *Do Not Disturb* and saved myself the headache. Would've saved me a trip to the Apple Store and a couple hundred dollars I ain't really want to spend. But I wasn't thinking straight. I've been on edge lately, snapping on everybody, and when you're on edge like that, you don't make the smartest decisions. Sex with Toot wasn't even getting rid of the edge, and when I'm hitting that, I fuck the dog shit out of her.

I had to make an appointment at the Apple Store for today, called in late just to get it fixed. *The Genius Bar*, they call it. Ain't nothing genius about paying damn near $300 to fix a screen I broke being in my feelings. If I had my son over the weekend like I normally do, crashing out wouldn't even been an option. I would have to keep my shit together for him. But I didn't have him. And if somebody asked me right now where my son was at or when I last talked to him, I wouldn't even have a good answer. And that's a problem. A big-ass problem for me.

***

Soon as I paid for the screen repair and picked up my phone from the tech at the *Genius Bar*, I turned it on. It looked like new. Notifications started flooding in, texts, missed calls, voicemails, all the shit from the past two days when my phone was out of commission. Most of them were from Sena's crazy ass trying to get through to me. A few from my mama asking if I was straight. One from my sister checking in on me.

Before I could even start scrolling through to see what else I missed, my phone started ringing right there in my hand. Unknown number.

"Man, hello," I answered, already irritated and ready to tell Sena about herself if this was her calling from some new burner number trying to get around me ignoring her ass.

"Sacavè, why the fuck are you ignoring my son?" Kia's voice came through that phone loud as hell.

"You sound stupid as fuck. Why would I do that?" I shot back.

The way Sena was blowing up my phone for two whole days, Saviour's calls probably wasn't even coming through. His attempts to reach me were probably getting buried under all her bullshit messages. And once my screen was cracked, I couldn't see nothing anyway, couldn't see who was calling, couldn't read texts, couldn't do shit. I would never deliberately ignore my son. But here go Sena affecting more shit in my life, causing problems even when she's not around. At this point, I might have to go ahead and change my number. Rekindling our friendship is completely out the question. That bridge is burned.

Kia ain't respond right away. All I heard in the background was muffled voices, her and that nigga going back and forth.

"Yo, man. It's Tool. What's up?" His voice came through, all calm like he trying to be the peacemaker.

"What's up," I answered dry, my jaw already tight as hell. Because I already knew if this nigga was about to get on my line and start talking to me about my son, shit was about to get real ugly real fast.

"Hear me out. I'm a man, and this is my wife. I don't disrespect her, and I'm not gon' allow nobody else to disrespect her either. With all due respect, Savy been asking for you, bro. As a mother, and a damn good one, her maternal instincts went off when she saw him upset asking about you. We can get on the next flight out of Paris if that's what she wants. We just tryna fix the problem, man. That's all this is," Tool continued.

It seems like I can't catch a break at this point. Now I can't even have a conversation with my baby mama without her new nigga inserting himself into the situation, acting like he got a say in my relationship with my son. I get that he married her. I get that he around Saviour now. But he ain't his daddy. I am. That's my blood.

"Put Kia on the phone," I demanded, leaving no room for discussion. I wasn't having this conversation with somebody I ain't make no baby with.

"She can hear you. You on speaker," he responded.

"Kia, bruh, this not what we 'bout to do," I pushed, trying to keep my voice level, not tryna come off too hostile but finding it hard not to when it came to my son.

If this conversation was gonna remain respectful, if it was gonna stay productive and not turn into some disrespect I ain't need to be talking to another man about my child. If Kia knew me like I believe she knew me, it was in her best interest to take the phone from that nigga and get it off speaker. This should be between me and her. Nobody else needed to be in this.

The line got quiet. I could hear them whispering to each other.

"Kia," I said louder, my tone making it clear I wasn't about to sit here and wait all day for her to make a decision.

"Sacavè, just call your son. Better yet, pick him up from school today. That would make his whole day," she finally responded.

"Bet," I said, then hung up before either one of them could say anything else. I ain't need no lecture. I ain't need no advice from them. I just needed to handle my business with my son.

***

I sat in my truck in the parking lot for a minute, scrolling through my notifications, swiping past all Sena's desperate ass messages until I saw the ones that made me feel like the worst father alive.

Five missed FaceTime calls from Saviour over the past two days. Three text messages.

hi dad

dad can u call me

i miss u

My son had been reaching out, trying to connect with me, and I ain't even see it because I was too busy crashing out over Sena's snake ass. Too busy being in my feelings about Kia moving on and getting remarried. Too busy drowning in my own problems to be there for the one person who actually needed me most and ain't do nothing to deserve being ignored.

I checked the time on my dashboard. 2:47 PM. School let out at 3:15. If I left right now and hit the highway, I could make it.

I started the truck and pulled out that parking lot ready to see my son's face. When I tried to pick him up Friday the school gave me hell. Said they had strict instructions to only release Saviour to the people on the approved checkout list, and apparently my name wasn't one of them. I'm still trying to wrap my head around when the checkout list went from the original four people, me, Kia, her mama, and her sister, to seven people that somehow don't include me, his own goddamn father.

But I wasn't about to make no scene. Not in front of them other boujee-ass parents and teachers at that expensive-ass private school.

***

I pulled up to Saviour's school at 3:10 PM sharp, found a parking spot close to the entrance, and made my way toward where all the parents waited for pickup. The school was really nice, one of them spots where tuition cost more than some people's rent. But it was worth every penny for the education Saviour was getting: the smaller classes, the individual attention from teachers who actually give a damn. Me and Kia had agreed on this school back when we were still together, back when we could still agree on shit without it turning into World War III.

A whole bunch of navy-blue pants and white polo shirts bundled up together, running to find their parents, nannies, whoever was there to pick them up.

And then I spotted Saviour walking next to his teacher.

He wasn't running like the other kids. He wasn't laughing and playing. Saviour was walking slow as hell. And no six-year-old should ever look like that. That shit broke me right there.

I was about to move toward him when he looked up. His eyes scanned the crowd of parents, probably looking for Kia's mama or whoever was supposed to get him today, and then they landed on me.

His eyes got wide, like he couldn't believe I was standing there. His mouth dropped open. And then his whole face lit up with pure joy, the kind you can't fake even if you tried, and he screamed at the top of his lungs, "*Dadddd.*"

He took off running toward me full speed like he was running the forty-yard dash.

"What's up, son?" I said, wrapping my arms around him.

"I missed you, Dad," he said, his voice muffled against my chest. He started crying. And that shit bothered me.

Nothing mattered more than this moment right here. Nothing felt better than holding my son, feeling him hold me back, like he was afraid if he let go I might disappear again. My decision not to keep Saviour during his mama's ten-day honeymoon because I was in my feelings, not answering his calls because my phone was fucked up, all that selfish and inconsiderate shit. It was hurting him. My son. The most important person in my whole life.

"I missed you more, son," I said.

We stood there for what felt like forever but was probably only a minute or two, just holding each other while other parents and kids walked past us going about their day. The teacher stood nearby.

"Stay right here for a second, a'ight? Let me go check in with the front office real quick so they know I got you and we straight to leave," I finally said.

"Okay, Dad," Saviour said, wiping his eyes with the back of his hand, trying to pull himself together.

***

Inside the main office, the secretary, the same white lady who had given me problems and attitude on Friday when I tried to pick Saviour up, was sitting at her front desk typing away on her computer. She looked up when the door opened and I walked in and put on this fake smile.

"Good afternoon. How can I assist you today, Mr. Sanders?" she asked, her tone way friendlier than it was last time.

"Yeah, do you mind pulling up and printing out that updated checkout list for me?" I asked.

"Sure, no problem. Let me just pull that right up for you," she said, turning back to her computer. Then she stood up from her desk and walked over to the printer on the other side of the office.

I watched her walk across that office. She was fine as hell, real put together and professional, looking. Pretty face, blonde, and a body that the school dress code couldn't quite hide. The type of woman who probably got hit on by single dads at this school on the regular, niggas trying to shoot their shot during pickup and drop-off just for a chance to get in her inbox.

She came back holding a printed sheet of paper and handed it to me with another one of them smiles. "Here you go. Is there anything else I can help you with today?"

"I'm picking up Saviour Sanders," I said.

"That's fine. You're on the list. His teacher will release him to you," she said back.

The way she said it, voice just a little softer than it needed to be, told me shawty might be offering more than just administrative help if I wanted it. But I wasn't interested. I had too much other shit going on in my life to even think about entertaining that. Plus, I never hit a snow bunny before. Ain't tryna be in no *Get Out* type situations.

"Nah, this is perfect. Appreciate it," I said, reading the paper without even bothering to walk away first.

It was an email. One that Kia had sent to the school. And reading it made me irritated.

***

To whom this may concern,

This email serves as an update to my request. While out of the country for 10 days, Saviour Sanders' checkout list be as follows:

Tonya Williams (grandmother) Tamia Williams (aunt) Vanessa Jackson (cousin) Tia Bell (aunt) Bernard Bell (uncle) Kristen Warren (grandmother) Robert Warren (grandfather) Sacavè Sanders (father)

***

I never in my entire life felt this tried. Not even the foul-ass shit Sena pulled forging my signature topped this moment right here, looking at this paper.

This new nigga must got Kia's head gone for her to really believe that his family members are about to be on my son's checkout list. Above my family. Above my mama who's been in Saviour's life since the day he was born. Above my sister who that boy loves like crazy. Above people who actually share blood with him, who was there before Tool even entered the picture.

And not only are they on this list, but I'm at the very bottom. Listed last. After everybody else, including people who just met my son almost two years ago.

Tool's parents, people my son barely know, can pick up my child from school, but my own mama can't? That's supposed to be the new reality now that she remarried?

"Yeah, this is perfect. Thanks," I said, folding that paper up and shoving it deep in my back pocket.

I know how to pick my battles. I know better than to completely lose my shit and black out in this white-ass establishment, in this expensive boujee private school. But best believe I'm definitely addressing this situation one way or another real soon.

***

Saviour was right where I left him, standing next to his teacher, bookbag on, holding his lunchbox. His eyes locked on me the second I came back through the door, and he grabbed his teacher's hand and pointed like he needed her to confirm I was real.

"He's all yours, Mr. Sanders," she said, nodding at me.

"Appreciate you," I said.

Saviour walked over and grabbed my hand without saying a word. Just grabbed it and held on. We walked out to the truck together like that.

I got him buckled in the backseat, tossed his bookbag in the trunk, and pulled out of the parking lot. For the first few minutes, neither one of us said anything. I could feel him looking at me from the backseat, though, that quiet six-year-old energy where they got questions but they waiting to see if you gon' bring it up first.

I brought it up first.

"Aye, I owe you an apology, son," I said, keeping my eyes on the road.

"For what?" he asked.

"For not answering when you called me. And for not calling you back," I said.

He was quiet for a second. "Why didn't you answer, Dad?"

I exhaled. How do you explain to a six-year-old that you threw your phone through a wall because you were in your feelings? You don't. But you don't lie to him either.

"My phone broke, son. The screen shattered and I couldn't see nothing on it, couldn't see calls coming in, couldn't read texts, couldn't do nothing. That's where I was today, getting it fixed. And I'm sorry it took me this long," I said.

"So you didn't see me calling you?" he asked, and the relief in his voice hit me somewhere I ain't expect.

"I didn't see it, Saviour. I promise you. If I woulda seen it, I woulda picked up every single time," I said.

"Okay," he said quietly.

"But listen to me. And I need you to really hear me on this," I said, glancing at him in the rearview mirror. "No matter what's going on with me, with your mama, with anything... I'm always gon' be your father. Always. You understand me? Ain't no situation, ain't no circumstance, ain't nothing in this world that's ever gon' change that. I'm not going nowhere."

He nodded, twisting the strap on his seatbelt the way he always did when he was processing something.

"Promise?" he asked.

"Promise," I said. "That's my word to you."

He looked out the window for a second. Then: "Dad, can we get Chick-fil-A?"

I laughed before I could stop myself. Six years old and already knew how to reset the energy in a room. "Yeah, boy. We can get Chick-fil-A."

***

"You got homework?" I asked Saviour soon as we walked through the front door of my crib, already knowing the answer but asking anyway.

"I-I did it in class," he answered quick, stuttering, which was usually a dead giveaway that he was lying.

"Yo-yo-you a lie," I called him out immediately, pointing toward the stairs. "Go do your homework before you even think about touching that game, boy. Don't play with me."

"But Dad—" he started to protest, trying that negotiation tactic kids always try.

"Ain't no buts. Homework first. You know what's up," I said.

It's like these kids forget we were their age once. They think they slick with it, like we don't know every trick in the book. "I did it in class" is one of the oldest lies in the whole parenting handbook. I tried that same exact line on my mama back in the day. And she used to hit me with her go-to response every single time: "If the teacher gave you homework, she wants you to do it at home. That's why it's called homework and not classwork." I would never forget them days her standing over me at the kitchen table making sure I finished every last problem, wouldn't let me get up until it was done right.

Now that I'm sitting here thinking about it, remembering how my mama used to handle me when I was being hardheaded, how she always knew exactly what to say to get through to me even when I was acting out and being stubborn, maybe she's the better person to talk to about all the bullshit that's been going on in my life lately. About feeling like I'm losing control of everything around me and don't know how to get it back. About this disrespectful-ass checkout list that got his family on it above mine. About how to be a better father when everything in my life feels like it's falling apart piece by piece.

My mama always kept it a hundred with me. Never sugar-coated shit, never told me what I wanted to hear just to make me feel better. She always told me exactly what I needed to hear, even when I ain't wanna hear it.

Chapter 15

"Bae, listen, we enjoyed five days in Paris already. If you want me to call and get our flights changed to the next thing smoking, I can do that. It's your world," Tool insisted.

Lord, thank you. I am so deeply grateful for and in love with this thoughtful and understanding man I married. I'm worried about my son, and to be honest, I'm worried about his father too. I could care less what's going on in his personal life up until it starts to affect my son, and he has come to that point. Let's just see what happens now that I added him back to the pickup list.

"No, baby. We can enjoy the rest of our trip. I'm enjoying you, and I want to keep enjoying you," I said, kneeling down in front of him.

I started pulling my hair back into a ponytail.

Tool looked down at me with that look, one that said he already knew exactly what time it was, and did as he was told.

I took him in my hand first, stroking slow, feeling him grow before I even put my mouth on him. I wanted him fully ready. Fully present. I looked up at him one more time before I wrapped my lips around the tip, nice and slow, letting him feel the warmth before I took more of him in.

Tool exhaled through his nose and his hand found the back of my head, not pushing, just sitting there. Like he needed something to hold onto.

I worked him like I had something to prove. Long, slow strokes with my hand while my mouth handled what it could, then I switched, taking more of him, letting him hit the back of my throat, holding it there just long enough to make him grip the sheets. I used my tongue on the underside the way I knew drove him crazy, flicking slow at the base before taking him all the way back in.

"Kia—" he started.

I didn't stop. I sped up. I pulled him deeper and let him hear how good he tasted because I wanted him to know this wasn't something I was doing. This was something I *wanted* to do.

When I felt him tense up, felt his thighs lock, heard the way his breath broke apart, I stayed right there. Hands on his thighs, eyes up, and I took everything he gave me without flinching.

I swallowed every bit of my man's kids, then got up and wiped my mouth. Swallowing his semen honored my religion. I love sucking the soul from a deserving man.

Tool pulled me up by my face and kissed me like I had just done something sacred.

"You trying to make me wife you twice?" he said against my lips.

"Already did," I said, smiling.

***

We spent the rest of that day doing absolutely nothing productive and everything intentional. We ordered room service and ate in bed, watched a French movie neither one of us could fully understand and laughed about it anyway, and eventually found our way back out onto the streets of *Paris* at night.

There was a wine bar a few blocks from the hotel that we had walked past every day and kept saying we would stop there. We finally did. We sat at a small table by the window for almost two hours, drinking on a bottle of something the server recommended that I couldn't pronounce, just talking.

Not about Sacavè. Not about Saviour's schedule or what we were coming home to. Just us and where we wanted to travel next, where we wanted to buy our vacation home, whether Tool thought Saviour would be tall like him one day.

"He already got big feet," Tool said.

"Don't put that on me. His daddy's feet are huge," I said.

Tool laughed. "Then he gon' be a giant."

It was easy. That's the part nobody tells you about finding the right person. No performance, no walking on eggshells, no wondering what mood you're about to walk into. Just easy.

***

We saved the *Love Lock Bridge* for our last full day in *Paris*.

I had seen it online months before the wedding: couples attaching padlocks to the bridge and throwing the key into the *Seine* as a symbol of their love being permanent and unbreakable. I thought it would be the cutest thing for us to do. I even bought some custom locks, had them engraved with our initials and our wedding date on one side and *Mr. & Mrs. Warren* on the other.

We walked to *Pont des Arts*, the *Seine* below us. I pulled the locks out of my purse and handed Tool his.

He turned it over in his hand, reading the engraving, and got quiet.

"You really thought of everything," he said.

"I try," I said, bumping his shoulder.

We found our spot on the railing, clicked our locks into place side by side, and I held both keys in my palm.

"You ready?" I asked.

"Always," he said.

We threw them together.

Tool put his arm around me and pulled me into his side.

"That's forever," he said.

"That's forever," I agreed.

***

The night before our flight, we went back to *Le Cinq*. Tool had wanted to end the trip the same way we started it. Fancy dinner, good wine, just the two of us. We toasted to the trip, to the marriage, to whatever came next.

Back at the hotel for the last time, I stood at the window looking at the city.

I was ready to go home. But I was going to miss this.

Tool came up behind me and wrapped his arms around my waist, resting his chin on my shoulder.

"You good?" he asked.

"More than good," I said. "Thank you for this."

"Thank you for being my wife," he said.

***

As much as I enjoyed Paris, I must say it felt good to be home.

I couldn't wait to see my son and feel my own bed. I couldn't believe I was actually married, happily married, to someone who enjoyed saying "my wife" just as much as I enjoyed saying "my husband." I was just happy to be doing marriage the right way. My in-laws were picking us up from the airport, and the only thing I was dreading was having to call Sacavè to tell him to bring Saviour home.

There had been a lot going on with him that I had put on hold while I enjoyed my honeymoon, and I was now being forced to face all of it. I also only had three more days off before I had to return to work. I couldn't say I was too excited about that either. But one thing at a time, as my husband would say.

I decided to call Sacavè first. When I did, I got a disconnection message. I panicked, then called Saviour.

"Hello," he answered, but he was clearly distracted by the game.

Son, I said, tapping on the screen. *Pause the game and pick up the phone.*

"Hey, Ma. Hey, Pops," he said, finally looking up and greeting both of us at the same time.

It was crazy how not too long ago I was Mommy, and now I was Ma. My baby was growing up way too fast on me. My in-laws had been teasing us, saying he was making room for his other siblings. Tool was a good stepdad and a good uncle. I honestly wouldn't mind it, but I also enjoyed having Tool all to myself right now.

"We're back from Paris. Auntie Tia and Uncle Nard just picked us up from the airport," I said excitedly.

"Hey, Auntie T. Hey, Uncle Nard." Saviour greeted them immediately, not missing a beat.

You couldn't tell him those weren't his blood. Our family had blended so perfectly. I always wanted a big family, so this warmed my heart completely. They had been trying to talk me into transferring Saviour to the same public school as Nala and BJ, too, but I wasn't sure I was ready to start exposing him to what public school had to offer. Everyone raised their kids differently these days, and I didn't need any of the corrupted ones corrupting my little sheltered baby.

"Are you coming home tonight or after school tomorrow?" I asked. That question was more for his dad than him, but I would rather he go ask.

"Umm, tonight. Please, Ma, please," he pleaded.

"Where's your dad? Go ask him if he minds dropping you off," I said.

Sacavè had declined dropping our son off. Saviour wanted so badly to come home, so I was about to go pick him up myself. Even though we were married, his dad still didn't want Tool to know where he lived, so I was making the drive alone. Tool was heading over to his place to unpack in the meantime.

I wasn't looking forward to interacting with Sacavè. He had become more and more irrational by the day.

***

When I got outside, I called Saviour to come out. He said his dad needed to talk to me.

I parked, got out, and took a deep breath, pacing myself for whatever I was about to walk into.

When I walked in, Saviour was still on the game.

"Is all your other stuff at Suga's or Auntie Tia's?" I asked.

"Suga's," he answered, still focused on the screen. "Dad is upstairs in his room, I think," he added.

"Boy, you better come show me some love before that game ends up in the trash," I demanded.

I missed my boy so much. Ten days felt like a year. He even looked an inch taller.

"Sacavè," I yelled out from the bottom of the stairs. Felt like I was calling out for my other son, big-ass kid.

He didn't answer. So obviously he wanted me to come up.

I stepped into the room and it felt like walking into a trap, it smelled like stale air and neglected hygiene. This grown-ass man looked like he'd been demoted to a teenager; he was literally the twin of the older son I never wanted. My eyes hit the drywall first, a jagged, ugly hole punched right into the middle of it, then scanned the overflowing laundry basket that looked like it hadn't seen a washing machine in weeks. And Sacavè was a wreck. No haircut, edges looking like a forest, and hella facial hair matted to his face like he'd forgotten what a razor felt like. He looked completely undone.

"What's up with you?" I said, the disgust written all across my face. "What's this?" I asked, pointing at the hole in the wall.

"That's the reason I couldn't contact my son. I threw my phone 'cause Sena kept calling it like a fucking lunatic," he answered. "And that's why I changed my number too."

"Ha." I blurted it out. I couldn't help it. Two years ago, I would've been tickled and antsy to hear about him and his side-bitch bestie's soap-opera bullshit, but today I am healed and happy and would rather be spared.

"Well, I still ask that you keep that dramatic, angry, crazy bullshit away from my son," I added.

"That's my son too," Sacavè responded.

I felt like I was in a banter with a child at this point. Like, *no shit, duh, he is your son too.* Unfortunately for me.

"Sacavè, are you serious right now?" I asked.

"I mean, I feel like this nigga got you delusional and you forgot that part. You got my son calling the nigga Pops, and then you took me off his checkout list to add this nigga's family like the tuition don't come out of my muhfuckin' account. So again, that's my son too," he said, slamming some papers down.

I started to read them. It was an email thread, one I had sent while in Paris, editing and updating my son's checkout list. One I never thought his school would print from the email itself and hand to Sacavè.

"First of all, watch your tone when you're talking to me. And no—"

He walked up to me and started backing me toward the wall like he was trying to intimidate me.

"Continue," he demanded.

"No one got Saviour calling them anything. He started that on his own. You were taken off the pickup list when you decided you didn't want to care for him the ten days we would be in Paris, so we had to make other arrangements," I said, pointing in his face as I spoke. "And of course you pay his goddamn tuition, he's your son."

I pushed him as soon as I finished what I had to say. He would've been through the wall had my son not been downstairs.

"All this 'we' shit, like you came back from Paris speaking French, is dead when it comes to my son," he said. "You felt your ways about Sena, but I never puppeted her in your face the way you doing with this nigga, Kia." His voice had shifted into something that sounded less like anger and more like actual pain.

I started to walk off. The conversation was clearly no longer about our son. But then he snatched my arm back and tossed me onto the bed.

"Sacavè," I yelled.

His eyes looked angry. Demonic, almost. It was nothing I had ever seen in all the years I had known him.

I hadn't meant to yell loud enough for Saviour to hear, but as soon as I did, I heard him come tearing up the stairs like he was taking them two at a time.

"Ma," Saviour called out.

"Savvy, me and your mother are talking. Go back downstairs," Sacavè demanded.

"Ma, are you okay?" he asked, ignoring his father completely.

"Yes, I'm fine," I responded, keeping my voice steady even though my heart was pounding.

"Saviour," Sacavè yelled.

"Don't fucking yell at my son, Sacavè. Control yourself," I said through clenched teeth. Then I softened my voice before it reached Saviour. "Saviour, we're just talking. I'll be down in a second. Go back downstairs."

I didn't take my eyes off Sacavè once.

Chapter 16

As soon as I heard Saviour's footsteps going back down the stairs, I continued.

"You most definitely paraded that bitch in my face. I was pregnant with her in my face, and she's been around us for years all while you told me she was your best friend. You end up fucking her. Or maybe you had been fucking her. Tool has never called your phone, pulled up to your job, put shit on your car, or kept Saviour's iPad. That man wouldn't even touch me as long as I was your wife. You started fucking her well before she even signed the divorce papers, so please," I said, frustrated, rubbing my now bruised arm.

"Me and Sena fucked, I can count on both hands how many times. We was not fucking like that," he added.

Just like a manipulator to pick the least important part to address, as if sex two or three times, or even just once, is appropriate with someone he told me was his best friend.

"Sacavè, listen. I don't give a fuck. I don't care," I insisted. "You win. This is water under the bridge."

"No, I lost. My family. My wife. My best friend. And now I feel like I lost my mind too." He paused, the words coming out slower now, heavier. "I spent the last year thinking I was getting over it and I'm not. It don't matter who's been around. I never intended on divorcing you because I was trying to be the man you need and deserve from me. I didn't tell Sena to do that shit, and she's dead to me for doing it. If I was a lame-ass nigga, she would be locked up right now," he pleaded. "I'm facing 'bout twenty blunts a day with no appetite because you married the next nigga, Ki."

The passion in his voice made me tear up. He had definitely lost some weight. He also seemed to have been losing himself as the wedding day came closer. For once, I believed something coming out of his mouth. I watched as he talked, lost for words, because the anger he had ten minutes ago had quickly converted to hurt.

"I didn't say no to watching or keeping Saviour to be spiteful. I didn't want my son to witness me lose my shit. He got my temper. I can't teach him how to deal with his when I can't even deal with mine," he said, sobbing. "I lost. And if I was weak, I would kill myself right here, right now. 'Cause I can't take it. I feel like I'm suffocating."

"Sacavè," I said, whispering, my tears starting to fall. His admission of contemplating suicide bothered me the most.

"On my son, Kia. I can't take it," he insisted. "The counselor's even frustrated with a nigga."

"You're in therapy?" I asked, shocked.

He nodded.

I broke. I reached in and hugged Sacavè, a real, wholesome, maternal hug, because it felt like he had been holding in every feeling until this very moment. He went limp into my arms like that hug eased something he had been carrying alone. I couldn't hold up the weight of it either, so we fell onto the bed and held each other as we both cried.

I jumped up as soon as I heard Saviour coming up the stairs.

"Ma, Pops said can you open the garage from your phone?" Saviour questioned through the door.

"Ye-yeah, I'm doing it right now. Is he on the phone?" I asked, concerned.

"No, he texted," he answered back.

I grabbed my phone and noticed a couple of missed calls and texts from Tool. I quickly wiped my tears and cracked the door. "Son, go take a shower and get ready for bed. It's past your bedtime."

"I—okay, Ma," he answered. He looked like he wanted to question why we were still here when the plan was to leave, but he didn't.

"I don't need to cut that phone off on my end, do I?" I asked as he walked off.

"No, Mother," he responded.

I didn't want to confuse Saviour. Or even Sacavè. But I just couldn't find in my heart to leave while he was in his current headspace. I was grateful my son didn't have any questions because I didn't have any answers.

As I turned around, Sacavè had his arms out, pulling me into another hug. Everything about the embrace felt wrong because I was between his legs with his head on my chest and his arms around my waist.

"Thanks for staying, Ki," he mumbled.

***

We sat like that for a while, neither one of us talking, both of us still processing everything that had just been said out loud for the first time. Then the silence cracked open and everything started pouring out, the real shit, the shit that don't make it into arguments because arguments aren't about the truth; they're about winning.

He told me he knew he had been selfish. That he spent so long trying to be strong that he forgot how to ask for help. That watching me move on felt like watching himself disappear in real time.

I told him I didn't want the divorce either. Not like this. Not the way it happened. That losing what we were supposed to be had left an ache that I tried to distract myself from with work, Saviour, and eventually Tool, but the bruise was still there underneath.

"I still love you, Ki," he said quietly. "I never stopped."

My tears came back. "I love you too, Sacavè. I'm always gon' love you. But loving somebody and being with them ain't always the same thing."

"I know," he said.

This was the man I had built a life with, made a child with, cried over, and healed from.

He wiped my face with his thumb. Then he kissed me.

What happened between us after that wasn't what I expected. It wasn't the rushed, guilt-driven thing it probably should've been. It was slow and familiar, his hands remembering exactly where to go, my body betraying every boundary I had built. He kissed my neck and then my collarbone.

"I missed you," he said against my skin.

I didn't answer. I just held him.

He made love to me like he was grieving and celebrating at the same time, like he was saying bye and holding on with everything he had. I felt every emotion he had confessed in every movement, and against every piece of better judgment I possessed, I gave him the same back.

Afterward, we laid there. He was out and in a deep, peaceful sleep. I lay there staring at nothing but darkness, laying in his arms.

I got up before the guilt could swallow me whole.

***

I did Saviour's laundry first, then Sacavè's. Then I cleaned the bathroom, wiped down the kitchen counters, swept the floor.

Somewhere between folding a load of Saviour's shirts and starting another, I cried while I stood at the washing machine at two in the morning, doing laundry in my ex-husband's house the night after my honeymoon.

I am no better than Sacavè at this point.

Tool had called twice. I stepped outside and called him back, whispering.

"I'm at my mother's doing Saviour's laundry. He left a bunch of stuff over there," I said.

"Why you whispering?"

"Everybody's asleep," I said.

"I can't sleep," he said. "Uncomfortable being away from my wife."

"I'll be home soon," I said. "Get some rest."

***

The next morning . . .

"Have a good day, Papa," I said to Saviour as he jumped out of the truck. "Love you."

"Love you too, Ma," he said, slamming the door.

My eyes were swollen from crying with Sacavè all night. I had barely gotten any sleep and, to make matters worse, I had fucked my ex-husband just hours after my honeymoon. I wouldn't even use the word fucked. It was lovemaking.

The sex is something Tool would not find out about unless I or Sacavè told it. And then I had to think about how I would explain my puffy, almost swollen eyes and the bruise on my arm.

As I pulled into my driveway, my phone dinged. A text from Sacavè popped up.

Thank you so much for last night. I feel a weight lifted off my shoulders. I appreciate everything you did around the house too. I miss everything about you. I love you.

Before I could reply and tell him it was all a big mistake and that all I wanted was healthy co-parenting between us, Tool came walking out with the biggest smile on his face.

Seeing that confirmed that what happened with Sacavè shouldn't have happened. Because this amazing man, who had recognized what he wanted right away, who had treated me right without question, who had gotten it perfectly on the first try, was not worth losing.

"Hey, ba—" he stopped and held my face.

"You been crying?" he asked.

"Yes," I answered calmly as he helped me out of the car.

We walked inside and he said nothing, just watched me, trying to figure out what I could've been crying about long enough to have my eyes this swollen, and why he hadn't heard it in my voice over the phone. Concern was written all across his face as I walked into the bathroom to shower. He followed me. I moved like he wasn't there.

"Kia . . . stop. For a second, just stop," he demanded, reaching for my arm.

I don't know what obsession everyone had with this arm, but I snatched it back with the quickness, then rubbed it.

"What happened to your arm?" he pressed.

"I hit it on the hook in the laundry room," I answered.

He looked at me strangely, like the answer wasn't good enough.

"Why are you looking at me like that?" I asked, getting naked.

"I'm trying to read my wife," he said. "Why you been crying?"

"The whole situation with Saviour and his dad. I don't know if his dad is losing his mind or what, but my son adores Sacavè. I don't want to be the reason he doesn't have a relationship with him," I answered.

I have no desire to be with Saviour's father. And making love to him last night had steered him in exactly the wrong direction. That may have been what he wanted, but for me, it was an impulsive and bad decision that I wanted to forget ever happened. His mental health matters to me because I love him as the father of my child, and I would be affected if he chose to take his own life. But that is not something I can fix on behalf of our relationship.

"I understand," Tool nodded. "Is it something you want to talk about?"

"Not really," I said, kissing him, then turning around and stepping into the shower.

As usual, my man stood outside the shower with my robe, holding it open for me to slide right in. He's so attentive. He would notice if my perfume changed. That thought alone made my stomach turn.

"I can pick Saviour up from school if you need to get some rest," he volunteered.

"I would love that. I just have to update the list again. He misses you," I said, forcing the excitement into my voice even as the guilt pressed down on me.

"Are you hungry?" he asked.

Something about him felt distant, like he was trying to make up for something. Or maybe it was just my guilty conscience making everything feel weird. Either way, all of it was too much for my brain to hold in a matter of twenty-four hours.

I definitely needed sleep.

Chapter 17

Tool

I was never really the type to just sit around the house doing nothing. Never been that nigga. Even on my off days, I needed to be moving, doing something with my hands, feeling productive. So, while Kia was knocked out getting the sleep she clearly needed, I went to the kitchen.

She had everything I needed. I was making my mama's smothered chicken, rice, and greens.

I had the chicken seasoned and in the pan, greens on low, rice going, the whole kitchen smelling like somebody's grandmother lived there, when my phone buzzed on the counter.

My mama.

"Hey, baby. Y'all get settled in?"

"Yes, ma'am. Kia sleep. I'm cooking."

"Already? Boy, you just got off a plane," she laughed.

"Can't sit still," I said.

"That's your daddy. Tell my daughter-in-law I called. And Tevin—"

"Yes, ma'am."

"I'm proud of you. Both of y'all."

"Appreciate that, Mama. Love you."

I hung up and went back to cooking. That's where my head was at, just the food, just the music coming low from my phone on the counter, just being home. Even after ten days in Paris, I missed just being in our space.

I gotta get Saviour from school later and let Kia rest. She needed it. Something was off with her since she got back from her mama's, and I wasn't gon' push, but I noticed. I always notice. That's just how I'm built when it comes to her.

***

Saviour came out the school doors and spotted my truck before I even had to text. He took off running, bookbag bouncing, and yanked the passenger door open.

"Pops."

"What's up, man? How was school?"

"It was good. We did a science experiment with baking soda and it exploded everywhere and got on Tyler's shirt," he said, already laughing before he even finished the sentence.

"Y'all blew something up?" I said, pulling off.

"Not like *blew up*, blew up. It just bubbled over. It was so funny though," he said.

I laughed. This boy stayed in something.

We rode for a minute, him talking about his day, the science experiment, something about a substitute teacher who didn't know nobody's name, a girl in his class who kept copying off him.

"You let her?" I asked.

He got quiet for a second. "A little bit."

"Saviour."

"She said she would give me her fruit snacks."

I shook my head, but I was fighting a smile. "That ain't the move, man. You worked hard for them answers. Don't be giving them away for fruit snacks."

"Yes, sir," he said, looking out the window.

Then after a second, he said, "I missed y'all when you was in Paris."

"We missed you too," I said. "You good though? Your grandma took care of you?"

"Yeah. And then I was at my dad's last night," he said.

I kept my eyes on the road. "Oh yeah?"

"Yeah, we was there when you texted me," he said. "She did all my laundry and made my bed and everything."

"That's your mama," I said, keeping my voice level. "Always taking care of everybody."

"Yeah," he agreed, already looking out the window at something else, done with the conversation like it was nothing.

I nodded slow and said nothing else.

He ain't know what he just handed me.

***

Kia told me she was at her mama's. Said everybody in the house was asleep, that's why she was whispering. Told me she was doing laundry.

Technically, she was doing laundry. Just not at her mama's house.

I wasn't gon' blow up. That ain't how I moved. But I was gon' find out what happened, one way or another, in my own time and in my own way.

"Aye," I said after a few minutes. "You know where we going?"

"Where?"

"Come see the new house."

His eyes went wide. "Okay."

"Yeah. Wanna see your room?"

"Yes," he said, excited.

The construction crew had knocked off for the day by the time we pulled up, so we had the place to ourselves. It was framed out, you could see the bones of everything, where the walls were gon' be, where the windows sat, how big the rooms were gon' feel when it was done.

Saviour walked through it with his mouth open.

I took him upstairs and showed him his room first. Big, with its own bathroom and a window seat that looked out over the backyard.

"This all mine?" he asked.

"All yours," I said.

He walked the whole perimeter with his arms stretched out like he was measuring it with his wingspan.

"Pops, this is big."

"You got room to grow," I said. "Come here, lemme show you something else."

I walked him back downstairs and out to where the backyard was marked off. Told him where the pool was going. Then back inside to the basement.

"Theater down here," I said, pointing. "Game room over there."

Saviour grabbed my arm. "A *theater*?"

"With the recliners and everything."

"Does Ma know about the theater?"

"Yup," I said.

He shook his head slow like it was too much to take in. "Nice."

I put my hand on his shoulder and we stood there for a second, just looking at the space. "You good with all of this? Me and your mama, the new house, all of it?"

He looked up at me. "Yeah."

"Okay, cool," I said.

He nodded, satisfied with that.

"Aye," I said. "Next year when you switch schools, you thinking about playing any sports? Nala and BJ be doing stuff over there."

Saviour thought about it for a second. "Basketball."

"Yeah? You know how?"

He immediately jumped as high as he could in the middle of the unfinished basement.

I laughed. "A'ight. We'll work on it."

***

When we got back to the house, the food was ready. Saviour dropped his backpack at the door and followed the smell straight to the kitchen.

"You cooked?"

"Go wash your hands," I said.

I fixed his plate and he went in. Kia had come downstairs by then, moving slow, still tired around the eyes. She kissed me on the cheek and fixed herself a plate without saying much. We ate together at the table, Saviour doing most of the talking, carrying the whole conversation the way he always did.

After he finished, he asked to be excused and disappeared upstairs to his game, and just like that, it was just me and Kia in the kitchen.

I watched her for a second. She was picking at her food, somewhere else in her head.

"Lemme ask you something," I said, casual, like it just came to me.

She looked up. "What's up?"

"Sacavè ever put his hands on you before?"

Something moved across her face. "No," she said. "And I don't play that. Why?"

"Just asking," I said, and took another bite like it was nothing.

She looked at me for a second like she was trying to figure out where that came from, then let it go.

I let her think she was in the clear.

But between what Saviour said in the truck and the bruise I already clocked on her arm when she got home this morning, my mind was already working. I wasn't gon' come at her sideways. That ain't how I moved. But I knew my wife.

And my wife wasn't telling me everything.

Chapter 18

Sacavè
2 Months Later

"So I got an idea for our next session," Britnie said.

I decided to keep seeing Britnie more frequently, even with the understanding from Kia that healthy co-parenting was all she wanted from me. My mental space is better than it was two months ago. I forgot who I was and I had to shake back. My baby mama is the only woman to ever witness me at that low. I hadn't even expressed the suicidal shit to Britnie; she probably would've referred me to a mental hospital. She definitely helps me express my thoughts better though. She's a good professional replacement for Sena. So basically, I'm paying for her to be my best friend. I could be tripping though, but sometimes I swear she was flirting back with a nigga.

"What is it?" I asked.

"We gon' meet up at *Wreck Room*," she said. "I think it would be real good for you. A rage room, you go in, you break shit, you let it out. Better stress reliever than anything you doing now."

"So you asking me on a date," I said, smiling.

"Call it whatever you gotta call it to show up," she answered, smiling back. "Next Wednesday cool?"

"I can't do Wednesday, but Friday, is Friday cool?" I said. "That's if my son can come."

Wednesday wouldn't work because I couldn't do it on my lunch break or before work without rushing the whole rest of my day, and after work didn't fit either because I pulled up to Kia's to spend my little time with Saviour and then prepared myself for the next day. Going into the weekend was better.

Plus, Saviour needed something like this too, honestly. He been spazzing out a lot lately. His teacher said the divorce could be affecting him more than he let on. He even got into his first fistfight the other day that almost got his ass expelled. Some little white boy called him a "wanna-be gangsta." That sounded a little too much like being called a nigga to me, so I didn't blame him, but I didn't tell him that. When I asked what made the boy even say that, Saviour said the little boy told him he smelled like weed.

Of course, Kia let me have it about that one. She went so hard. I don't even smoke no more, and smelling like weed don't even make you a gangsta. That lil' cracker been at home watching too many movies. Saviour is a smart kid, super proper lil' nigga, so smart they skipped him from kindergarten. I don't want him off track in that way.

"Even better, I would love to meet him," Britnie agreed. "Friday at four, assuming he'll be out of school by then?"

"For sure," I said.

***

I been calling out and coming in late so much these past three months everybody at work was tired of me. Part of it was how I felt about the whole remarry situation, and part of it was the new schedule they put me on. I'm a good worker though, so it was easy for my boss to go with the flow. Kevin, a cool old head. He filled me in on all the game about peace, marriage, and stability. He said counseling was bullshit. A scam to make money, a waste of time, all I needed was to spend some days with him.

But he was still cool with me coming in late on Wednesdays as long as I got back to myself and as long as I kept him updated on what Ms. Britnie's fine ass had on.

The Wednesday before Thanksgiving a couple weeks back was a blackout day. Couldn't come in late, so our session was on *Zoom*. You would've thought all the niggas in the break room needed therapy the way they was acting. Thirsty ass niggas.

Wait 'til I tell 'em she asked me on a date.

"Kev-O," I greeted, finding him in the break room pouring his coffee like clockwork. "What's up witcha, old head?"

"Shiiit, another day . . . another dolla. You seen my girl today?" he asked, right on cue.

I started laughing. "Yeah, man."

"What she talking 'bout?" he asked, leaning against the counter.

One thing about it: he didn't agree with paying somebody to tell him how to handle his life. Let him tell it. But he always wanted a full rundown after every session and agreed with damn near everything she said.

"She said I been making progress, holding myself more accountable. Said the next step is getting my anger out physically instead of just talking about it, so she wanna take me and Saviour to a rage room. You go in and just break shit, plates, bottles, whatever. Let it all out," I said.

"Oh yeah, and she right too, 'cause all that shit you been sitting on gotta go somewhere or it gon' eat you alive," he said, nodding slow. "Her fine smart ass," he mumbled into his coffee cup.

"Sound like a date," I added, like a proud teenager.

She said call it whatever I wanted to call it, and that's what I was going with. It ain't in that office. It's at another establishment. That's a date with Saviour coming too, so technically it was a family outing.

"Oh yeah. That's right too, nephew," he said, dapping me up. "She been batting them eyes at you enough anyhow," he joked.

"Feel me?" I said.

I just didn't know if it was part of her job or what. I probably wasn't the only nigga that had to get his life back intact that was getting batting eyes, rage room dates, and a little flirt. But a nigga was gon' take it regardless.

***

"Hello, Mr. Sanders, how are you?" the secretary asked when I walked in.

"I'm good, just doing a drop-in," I answered.

"Oh well, Saviour is pretty busy with visitors today, heh? Mr. Warren just left out not too long ago!" she said, all perky about it.

Shit made me cringe.

I just nodded. I didn't need no help being my son's father. My new work schedule had really turned me into a weekend dad whether I wanted it to or not. I worked four tens now, off Friday, Saturday, Sunday. I appreciated the extra day, but now I couldn't pick Saviour up from school like I used to. Ever since his teacher flagged his behavior, I tried to pop in when I could. Sit in his class, do him like my mama used to do me when I was cutting up.

Me and Kia agreed he would transfer to public school for third grade, but if he didn't get his act together, he staying his privileged ass at this preppy private school with these lil' white muhfuckas who thought he was a gangsta.

"Sign in right here. Here's your visitor sticker, Dad," she said.

And when she said *Dad*, all I could think about was what the fuck she called that nigga who thought he could do pop-ups at my son's school like he was the one who put in the work.

Chapter 19

"I don't know, baby. I think that sushi gave me food poisoning or something," I complained to Tool as I walked to my truck.

I decided to call it a day at work after I threw up what felt like my entire insides. I tried a new sushi spot near my job for lunch and, boy, was that a bad idea. Made it so bad. I had only been at work for an hour, eating it on my unofficial lunch break at my desk, and now I was trying to make it home before I had to throw up again.

"You need me?" he asked.

"I don't think so. I just need to get home right now. Oh my God," I complained.

"A'ight, call me if you do. This muhfucka just wrecked a forklift, I got a report to do," he responded, slightly irritated.

I'm sure my job thought I was full of shit, too, on top of all the vacation days I've been taking and all the ones I had coming up; now I was leaving sick on my office day. Thing is, if I had been home, I would've cooked, and sushi wouldn't have been tearing up my insides like this. I planned to clock back in when I got there, but the way I was feeling, it wasn't over when I got home either. I was contemplating the hospital. This sushi spot honestly should be shut down and reported to the *Better Business Bureau* the way I'm feeling.

***

After pulling over and throwing up again before making it home, I decided I needed a paper trail for this lawsuit I was about to file. I headed to the emergency room.

"What's your name?" the triage nurse asked.

"Kia Nichelle Warren," I answered.

"What brings you in today?"

"Food poisoning. I had sushi and it must've been bad because I feel terrible. I threw up three times already," I answered, feeling another one threatening to come up.

"Any diarrhea, nausea before eating, cramping, fever, or chills?" she probed.

"No, not yet at least. It's only been about an hour since I ate it," I answered.

***

After spending what felt like forever at that hospital, I was finally headed home. Saviour got picked up by his Suga, so I at least had some time to get some rest until Tool got off.

Turns out I wouldn't be doing any suing. Because I didn't have food poisoning.

I'm pregnant.

The nurse started off by telling me that with food poisoning, throwing up is usually followed by diarrhea. When she asked could I be pregnant, I told her I didn't doubt it. So she suggested labs, just to come back and say, *Well, baby, it ain't the sushi.* I hadn't even realized my period hadn't come. Between Saviour fighting at school, newlywed life, Sacavè's new schedule, building our new home, and living out of two houses, I just hadn't noticed.

Tool was so excited when I told him; he wanted to leave work right then, but couldn't. The nurse did an ultrasound to confirm and requested I follow up with my OB/GYN. At nine weeks, everything looked good.

I can't say I was shocked. Tool and I been fucking like rabbits, and our honeymoon was when we stopped using condoms. “I’m not fucking my wife with a condom, I need to feel what’s mine,” were his exact words. I also remembered plenty of nights where I moaned “cum in me, daddy”, part meaning it, part too caught up being his personal freak, so I was partly to blame. Although I would’ve loved to have him all to myself a little longer, I was excited about this journey with my husband. He was a great father figure to my son and his nieces and nephews, so I had no doubt he would be an even better father to our little one.

I called my OB/GYN to make an appointment, and Tool was already planning to call in late so he could be there. That alone was different from my original experience.

***

Christmas was just a few days away and I was doing my usual last-minute ripping and running to get gifts. Tool and I decided to announce the pregnancy on Christmas Day. Currently, nobody knew, not even Saviour, and it had been four weeks since I found out. We had been running the food poisoning excuse, and I felt bad putting a bad name on that sushi spot because, honestly, the sushi was good. Them bad reviews were just temporary.

I also had a feeling we were having a girl because I did not have morning sickness at all with my son. Barely had any symptoms at all. I was four months when I found out I was pregnant with him, and that was only because on top of all the crying I was doing, all I ever wanted to do was sleep and eat crab rangoons from *Main Moon*. To this day, Saviour loved crab rangoons.

For Christmas, we would just be visiting all our families and announcing. Saviour is going to be with Sacavè for the entire winter break, so I would bring his gifts from us and everyone else to him and tell him he was gonna be a big brother after break was over.

I was worried about this split household and how it was affecting Saviour. Sacavè mentioned he had taken him to the rage room with his therapist, and when it came to Saviour releasing his frustrations, he appeared extremely angry.

***

A Few Days Earlier — Sacavè

"Aye, man, we going to something called a rage room with one of my lady friends. That cool?" I asked.

"What's a rage room?" Saviour asked, already trying to Google it.

"She says it's a stress reliever. I've never been either, so I don't know, I looked it up. I think you just break shit," I answered.

Saviour shrugged. I wasn't stressed or angry at six years old. I was living my happiest young life that my mother could provide, and I wanted the same for my son. My father chose the streets over his family. My mother was left to play both sides, and I think she did an OK job. If I acted out, it could've been blamed on not having a father figure around in my teen years. I became an outstanding member of the neighborhood, rolling *60s* at a young age. Let's just say I didn't play.

If temper was hereditary, Saviour definitely got it from me. When Kia got mad, she didn't get angry. That was all me.

***

"Hey, you must be Saviour?" Britnie asked, reaching her hand out to shake his.

That was the most laid-back I had ever seen her. She had on some flare jeans that gripped that ass just right, a T-shirt, and some *Dunks*. The switch-up from her normal professional wear was sexy.

"Yes," he said, barely looking up from his phone, shaking her hand with his other one.

"I take it Dad didn't tell you about my no-phone policy," she said, looking over at me. "Yes, here too," she added.

I laughed. No woman had been able to make me wanna listen since Kia.

"Savy, go put our phones in the glove box," I said, handing him my phone and the truck keys.

"You look good on some chill shit without that notepad," I said as he walked off.

"Thanks. It's in my purse, actually," she said, laughing. "I mean, I can pull it out if you need me to."

I just shook my head because I believed her. Saviour came back and we walked toward the front desk where I heard nothing but noise, all kinds of slamming and smashing and breaking. Britnie led the way. The way my PTSD was set up, all that noise made me wanna reach for my hip.

"I got a season pass, he's my guest, and I'll pay for the little one separately," she told the cashier.

"I'll pay for Saviour," I butted in.

She gave me a stare that said, *No, you won't.* I backed down and gave her that. That authority made my dick stiff.

"How old is he?" the cashier asked.

"He's six," Britnie answered.

The cashier handed over three wristbands and a receipt. She put one on Saviour first, then came over to me.

"It's my job to remember these things, Mr. Sanders. Quit with the googly eyes," she said as she put my wristband on. She read my mind and all I could do was grin like a *Cheshire* cat, as my mama would say. The fact that we talked about me more than we talked about my son for her to remember that, that was attractive. After that, she handed me hers and I put it on, still smiling.

***

We went into different rooms with bats and poles, basically whatever we could get our hands on, and smashed everything in sight. Saviour took a real liking to breaking shit. Almost too much. But as long as it wasn't the stuff in my house, he could have at it.

The anger was shocking, though. And when the tears started to well up in his eyes, it caught me off guard. Britnie walked over to him. When I tried to approach, she held her hand up. I stopped in my tracks and watched.

"Tell me what you're feeling right now," she said to Saviour.

He quickly wiped his eyes.

"It's okay to cry. It's okay to be frustrated. But tell me why," she probed. "You upset at something specific?"

Saviour shook his head, then looked over at me. I felt glued to my spot until Britnie signaled me to walk over. When I got to him, my son wrapped his arms around me and started crying, his muffled words coming out against my chest.

"Sorry, Dad."

I was confused. Britnie backed away from us like she knew it was a moment she didn't need to be a part of. I didn't know what my son felt the need to apologize to me for. Even when I expressed how disappointed I was about him fighting at school, he didn't apologize then. He had his chin up and chest out like he hadn't done a thing wrong.

"You can't leave," Saviour said, looking over at Britnie.

Me and her both looked at each other, confused. He was still holding me when he said it, so I pulled his head back to make eye contact.

"Talk to me, son. What's going on?" I asked.

"Ma left, then TT Sena left. I don't want her to leave you alone, too," he said.

I looked over at Britnie, who had her hand over her mouth. And honestly, I felt the same way. I was lost for words. I wanted to say Sena ain't leave, I did the leaving, but that wasn't important right now. My son thought I was a lonely-ass nigga and he felt bad for me.

"So, Saviour, are you saying you're upset because your dad is alone?" Britnie asked, walking over.

"Yes." He nodded. "Everything is different now. Ma got Pops and he don't got TT Sena, so he been angry and mean."

I never meant to project how I had been feeling onto my son. I didn't feel like I had been mean to him. I just had to get more stern because Kia was on my ass like I was the reason he was tripping. When the teacher had that conference and mentioned the divorce, we both disagreed because he hadn't seemed affected. Apparently, he was.

"I'm the one that's sorry then. I'm the one that needs to apologize. I didn't realize I was being that way. I'll work on it," I said.

Raising my son had always been about breaking generational curses. I always wanted him to have an opinion, feel comfortable expressing it, feel like he could come to me about anything in this world. And I knew that as a parent, an apology to your child was okay. It didn't make you less of one. Sometimes being wrong was okay.

Britnie nodded, looking more proud than I had ever seen her. Any other time in that office, she acted like a nigga was stressing her out.

"You forgive me?" I said, dapping Saviour up.

He nodded.

"You heard him, Britnie? You can't leave me," I said, putting on a fake sad face.

Saviour didn't even know he just got me up about twenty points. I got a son, a best friend, and a wingman all in one.

"Sacavè, please," she said, calling me by my first name for the first time and rolling her eyes playfully.

Chapter 20

Christmas Day

We all settled around the table the way this family did, kids at their own table, adults packed into the dining room, everybody talking over everybody else.

Ms. Kristen had loosened up with me since the wedding. She hugged me now, real ones. Robert still wasn't a hugger, but he called me "baby," and that was enough. I had earned my place in this family and I could feel it in how they moved around me now. Like I had always been here.

Ms. Kristen don't play about Christmas. That house was decked out from the front door to the back: garland on the staircase, a tree that had to be pushing nine feet, candles on every surface, and that kitchen was doing the absolute most in the best way. Ham, mac and cheese, greens, cornbread, yams, potato salad, she had been in there since yesterday and it showed.

Honeygram was already in her chair by the tree when we walked in, hair pinned up, dressed like she was going somewhere after this even though she wasn't going nowhere.

"There go my grandbaby's wife," she said, arms already open.

Nala came flying down them stairs with BJ two steps behind her, both of them still in pajamas.

"Auntie Kia." She had my hand before I even got my coat all the way off.

"Girl, let her breathe," Tia said from the kitchen doorway with a mimosa already in her hand. "Merry Christmas, sis."

Nard came out behind her and hugged me over Tia's shoulder. "Welcome to the madness," he said.

The house filled up fast after that. Tajah and Fidel pulled up about an hour later, married now, courthouse ceremony two months before our wedding. Fidel had proposed the night of our engagement party. Tajah never let nobody forget that.

"He was inspired," she stayed saying.

Cool brought his girlfriend, Destiny. I met her briefly at the reception but didn't really get to talk to her. She was sweet, quiet, stayed close to Cool all night. Toot and Von came in loud as always, Von already into the eggnog before he said hey to anybody. Felicia was there with her daughter, Camille, who I was meeting for the first time; she missed the wedding because she was overseas. Tank brought his wife, Miss Debbie.

Then there was Jerome and Diane, Robert's brother and his wife. I met them at the wedding but didn't spend no real time with them. Jerome looked just like Robert, same quiet energy, same watchful eyes. Diane was the complete opposite; all warmth and words, already inviting me to their New Year's Eve dinner before I even got situated good.

It was a full house. Loud and warm and full.

***

We all got around the table the way this family did, kids at their own table, adults packed into the dining room shoulder to shoulder, everybody talking over everybody else. Tool had his hand on my thigh the whole dinner, same as always.

When things settled into that after-meal slowness, Tool squeezed my hand under the table. I looked at him. He nodded. I took a breath and looked around the table.

"We got something to tell y'all," I said. The table took a breath. "Y'all, we got something to tell y'all."

The table got quiet.

"We're pregnant."

Kristen screamed first, a full, from-the-gut scream that scared Robert and was around that table before I could even stand up. Tia was right behind her, mimosa still somehow in her hand. Honeygram clasped both hands together and said "Thank you, Jesus" three times. Diane grabbed Jerome's arm. Miss Debbie let out that laugh. Felicia started crying immediately and then tried to act like she wasn't.

But in the middle of all of it, I caught Kristen's face do something. She pulled me into another hug right after and it was real, I could feel that, but something was sitting underneath it.

***

I was helping Kristen in the kitchen when I noticed Robert pull Tool quietly into the hallway. Tia noticed too, caught my eye from across the counter, and shrugged like she didn't know either.

They were in that hallway for a minute.

When Tool came back into the kitchen, he kissed the side of my head and grabbed a piece of cornbread off the stove like nothing happened.

"You good?" I asked.

"Yeah, baby. I'm good," he said.

I left it alone. For now.

***

Kristen

I watched my son walk back into that kitchen smiling and my heart was doing two things at the same damn time. Soon as I could, I pulled Robert back into that hallway.

"Robert, we need to tell him," I whispered.

"Kristen." That voice. Firm and gentle, the same way it had been for thirty-something years.

"He got a right to know. That diagnosis—"

"Babe." He took both my hands the way he always did when he needed me to hear him. "He chose her as his wife. That's his family now. This is his moment. You tell him something like that today, on Christmas, in the middle of all this joy, he gon' be mad at you for it."

"But what if that baby—"

"I had the same condition," Robert said quietly. "And you standing here. And so is Tevin. And so is the rest of them." He looked at me. "Let them have this."

I pressed my lips together and looked back toward the kitchen where I could hear Kia laughing at something Tia said. She was good for my son. Anybody with eyes could see that. He was settled in a way I ain't seen him be in years, and she was the reason. But still.

***

Kia

We left from with his family and drove over to Sacavè's to drop off Saviour's gifts. I left Tool in the car and walked up to the door. Sacavè still didn't want Tool knowing where he stayed, so that was just how it was for now.

I barely got to the door before Saviour swung it open.

"Ma. Merry Christmas." He hit me full speed with a hug.

I grabbed him and squeezed him tight. I had been missing my baby something serious.

"Merry Christmas, boy. Where all this energy coming from?" I said, laughing.

"Come see what Dad got me." He was already pulling me inside. Then he stopped and looked past me toward the driveway. "Where's Pops?"

"He's in the car," I said.

Saviour's face did something quick. "How come he ain't come in?"

"Boy, go show me what your daddy got you," I said, redirecting him before he could go any further with it.

Marlene met me in the front room smelling like perfume and sweet potato pie, hugging me before I even got all the way settled. Faith was right behind her with Malik on her hip. They pulled me in like I was still family, always did, didn't matter what had gone on between me and Sacavè.

I set the gifts down and Saviour started sorting through them, calling out names like a lil' elf. I caught Marlene lean over to Faith and say something low. Faith glanced at my stomach then back at her mama, and they did that thing where they communicated a whole conversation with just their eyes.

I kept it moving like I didn't see.

Sacavè came downstairs minutes later, fresh cut, looking more like himself. Whatever he been doing these past two months was agreeing with him.

"Merry Christmas," I said.

"Merry Christmas," he said back. "Tool outside in the car?"

"Yeah—"

"He can come in," Sacavè said.

I looked at him. "Sacavè—"

"It's Christmas, Kia. I ain't gon' have that man sitting outside in the cold," he said.

I didn't know what to do with that version of him, so I just nodded and texted Tool.

"Hey," I said while we waited. "Sena reached out."

Sacavè's jaw tightened. "For what?"

"She got a gift for Saviour. I told her he was with you so she could just bring it here," I said.

"Why would you do all that?"

"Because she asked and it made sense—"

"You gave her my address?"

"Sacavè, get over it," I said. "She did us both a damn favor. Our marriage was already over whether she signed them papers or not, and you know that just as well as I do. Let. It. Go."

He looked at me for a minute. Didn't say nothing.

"Cool," he said. "She can bring it."

***

Sena showed up about an hour later. I answered the door and she looked different. Face fuller. Coat open. And underneath it, her stomach was very clearly not the stomach I remembered the last time I saw her.

She was pregnant. Not a little pregnant, almost *due* pregnant.

I stepped aside without a word. Sacavè came into the front room and stopped cold. They looked at each other with a whole year of everything just sitting right there between them.

Saviour ran in, saw her, and lost his whole mind.

"TT Sena." He wrapped his arms around her careful when he spotted the belly. "You got a baby in there?"

"I do," she said, laughing.

I watched Sacavè go through about fifteen emotions in thirty seconds. Then something in him just settled. Like he put something down he had been carrying too long.

"You good?" he said to her.

"I'm good, Cavé," she said softly.

And just like that, not all the way, but just like that, something cracked open between them two that had been sealed shut for over a year. I didn't need to be in the middle of none of that. I took myself to the kitchen with Marlene and Faith and let them have that.

***

By the time Tool came in, the whole vibe had shifted into something that almost felt normal. Sacavè met him at the door, not warm, not cold, just civil, shook his hand, and that was it. Saviour snatched Tool's arm before he could even get situated good and dragged him to the living room to run through everything he had gotten.

Marlene looked at me from across the room. I smiled at her. She smiled back.

And I just stood there in my ex-husband's living room on Christmas Day, nine weeks pregnant, watching my husband and my son on that couch together, trying to stay in the gratitude and not think too hard about everything sitting just below the surface of all of it.

Chapter 21

Sena

I almost didn't reach out. I went back and forth about it all morning, had Kia's name pulled up in my phone probably four times before I actually hit send.

Hey. I know it's Christmas and I know this might be weird, but I got something for Saviour. Is he with you?

I put the phone down and went back to doing nothing, which was basically all I could do these days. Eight months pregnant and my whole body had decided it was done cooperating with me. My back hurt, my feet were swollen, and I couldn't get comfortable sitting, standing, or laying down. I didn't know how women did this multiple times voluntarily.

My phone buzzed.

He's with his dad. New house on Cascade. You can bring it there if you want.

I stared at that for a minute.

Is he still mad at me?

The three dots popped up, disappeared, came back.

I don't know, Sena. But I'm married now. And pregnant. He don't know about the pregnant part, so just keep that between us.

I read that twice.

I've done enough damage. That ain't mine to tell. Congratulations, Kia. For real.

She sent back a simple heart and that was that.

***

I sat with that conversation for a minute before I finally got up, got myself together the best I could given that I looked like I was smuggling a basketball under my shirt, grabbed Saviour's gift, and got in the car.

The whole drive over I kept running through what I was gon' say. Or if I was gon' say anything at all. Maybe I would just drop the gift, say Merry Christmas, and keep it pushing. No need to make it more than what it was.

But then Kia answered the door and something about seeing her face just made everything feel less heavy than I expected. She looked good. Happy in a way that sat different on her than it used to. She stepped aside and let me in without making it weird, and I appreciated that more than she probably knew.

And then Sacavè walked up.

He stopped. I stopped. Saviour broke the whole moment by screaming my name and throwing himself at me, careful when he saw my stomach, and for a few seconds, that was the only thing happening in the room.

When I looked back up at Sacavè, the anger I expected wasn't really there. He looked tired more than anything. Tired and older than I remembered, even though it had only been a year.

"You good?" he said.

Two words. But coming from him, after everything, that was a lot.

"I'm good, Cavé," I said.

And something in him just . . . let go. I could see it happen.

***

We didn't hash everything out that day. Wasn't the time or the place for all of that with Saviour running around and Kia and Tool there and Marlene and Faith in the kitchen. But before I left, Sacavè walked me to the door and we stood there for a second, just the two of us.

"I'm sorry," I said. "I know I said it in them texts and them calls you ain't answer, but I need you to hear me say it."

He nodded slow. "I hear you."

"I never meant for any of it to go that far. I thought I was helping and I was wrong and I'll carry that," I said.

He looked at me for a long moment. "How you doing? For real."

"Scared," I said honestly, looking down at my stomach. "But okay."

"Who—" he started.

"Nobody you know," I said before he could finish.

He didn't push it.

"You got people around you?" he asked.

"My mama. My daddy. My sister," I said. "I'm okay."

He nodded again. "A'ight."

***

It's crazy how things work out sometimes. I was the one who tore them apart, and Kia, she rekindled us. Our friendship. Without even trying to.

I wasn't gonna fake like I wasn't the reason everything fell apart. I owned that. I been owning it every single day for the past year. But I also knew Sacavè well enough to know that marriage had been cracking before I ever did what I did. I just handed it the final push it needed to fall.

Sacavè told me he was in counseling now and I loved that for him. He was the type to get to a low place and just disconnect from everybody, even the ones that loved him most. Maybe she could help him deal with that better than he ever had on his own. Lord knows I tried for years to be that for him. You can't be somebody's therapist and their best friend at the same time. I learned that the hard way.

Being pregnant now, I understood Kia on a whole different level. How it could have you not wanting to do a single thing. How emotional everything became. How your body stopped being your own. I thought about her doing this with Sacavè, doing it mostly alone because he was locked up, and I understood the exhaustion she used to carry that I didn't always have grace for back then.

And I loved how she moved after. How she came out of all of it and got exactly what she wanted in less time than it took with Sacavè. That right there was the definition of "if he wanted to, he would." Tool wanted to. Simple as that.

I missed Saviour's sixth birthday because Sacavè ignored me day and night during that whole stretch. I kept up with Saviour through Kia's *Facebook*, the one she never removed me from, which still surprised me every time I opened it. Every time she posted something I felt like would hit Sacavè hard, I reached out to him. He never responded. His own page was basically dead except for the reels he reposted, depressing ones mostly, the kind that told you everything about where somebody's head was without them having to say a word.

When he changed his number on me, I charged the friendship to the game. Told myself that was it, that I needed to accept what I did and accept losing him as the consequence.

But then Christmas happened.

Chapter 22

Sacavè

"So, how you been since our last session?" Britnie asked, crossing her legs.

"Better than I been in a minute, honestly," I said. And I meant it. Christmas had done something to me I ain't expect. Seeing Sena, squashing that, watching Saviour light up, something about all of it just shifted something in me.

"Better how?" she pressed. She never just took "better" at face value. Always wanted the details.

"Like I can breathe," I said. "I ain't been able to say that in a long time."

She nodded slow, writing something down. "Talk to me about Christmas."

"She pulled up with her husband," I said.

"And?"

"And I handled it," I said. "Shook his hand. Let him come in. Kept it civil."

She looked up from her notepad. "That was big, Sacavè."

"I know."

"How did it feel in the moment?"

I thought about it for a second. "Like I was making a choice instead of just reacting. That's new for me."

She smiled at that. Not the professional smile she kept in the office; a real one. "That's the work showing up," she said.

I ain't gon' lie, hearing her say that hit different than I expected. I wasn't used to being told I did something right when it came to all this emotional shit. Most of my life the message was *shake it off, man up, keep it moving*. Sitting in this office twice a week and actually being told, *Yeah, you handled that*, that was still something I was getting used to receiving.

***

"Saviour been asking to go back to the rage room," I said.

Britnie's eyebrows went up. "Has he?"

"Every other day. Talking about can we go back, can he bring his friend next time," I said. "Got me thinking maybe I need to invest in one of them season passes."

She laughed. "It clearly resonated with him. That's actually really good to hear. Sometimes kids need a physical outlet for things they don't have the vocabulary for yet."

"He definitely ain't got the vocabulary for it," I said. "But he got the anger for it."

"He got it from somewhere," she said, giving me that look.

"Here we go," I said.

"I'm just saying," she said, holding her hands up.

***

"Can I ask you something about the rage room?" she said after a minute.

"Go ahead."

"The moment with Saviour when he broke down and apologized to you, when he said he didn't want me to leave you alone." She paused. "How did that land for you after the fact? When you had time to sit with it?"

I leaned forward, elbows on my knees. "Fucked me up," I said, honest. "My son out here feeling sorry for me. Six years old carrying my weight. That ain't his job."

"No, it's not," she said. "But the fact that he felt safe enough to say it and the fact that you responded the way you did, with accountability, with an apology, that's not nothing. A lot of fathers would've deflected. You didn't."

"I wasn't raised to apologize to nobody," I said. "Definitely not my kids."

"But you did it anyway," she said. "Why?"

"Because he deserved it," I said.

She nodded and wrote something down. Looked like she was trying not to smile too hard. "You know I'm proud of you, right?"

"You say that like I'm one of your kids," I said.

"Occupational hazard," she said. "You all become my kids eventually, whether I want you to or not."

I let that sit for a second. Then I said what I'd been turning over in my head since the rage room.

"Aye, let me ask you something," I said.

"Okay," she said, settling back.

"The rage room, that was outside this office. Different setting, different energy." I paused. "You told me to call it whatever I needed to call it to show up. I called it a date. You ain't correct me."

She tilted her head just slightly. Not giving me nothing yet.

"So I'm asking you officially," I said. "Not as my therapist. As Britnie. You wanna go on a date with me?"

The office got quiet for a second.

She uncrossed her legs. Crossed them the other way. Looked at me with that expression I still hadn't fully learned how to read after all these months.

"Sacavè—"

"Before you say no," I said, "just know I already thought through every reason you're about to give me."

"Is that right?" she said.

"*HIPAA*. Ethics board. Professional boundaries. All of it," I said. "I heard you. I'm still asking."

She was quiet for a minute. Her eyes did something. That told me enough.

"If I said yes," she said slowly, "it would have to be one or the other. Professional or personal. Not both. I can't be your therapist and your—" she paused, choosing her word, "—whatever else."

"So then no more therapy?" I asked.

"I would refer you to a colleague I trust," she said. "Someone good."

"And then?" I said.

She looked at me. "And then we would see."

"That's a yes," I said.

"That's a maybe," she said. "Don't push it."

I leaned back. "I'll take a maybe."

She shook her head and picked her notepad back up like she was trying to get herself together. "Can we get back to the session, please?"

"We can do whatever you want, Britnie," I said.

"Britnie," she repeated, looking up. "You keep using my first name."

"You keep letting me," I said.

She pressed her lips together to keep from smiling and lost the battle.

Chapter 23

One Week Later
Kia

I had been planning this moment since before Christmas. *Pinterest* had me going down a rabbit hole at two in the morning one night, looking at ways people announced pregnancies to their kids, and I finally landed on something simple enough not to be corny but cute enough to be a memory.

I ordered Saviour a shirt that said *Big Brother Loading...* on the front and had it wrapped up in a box with some of his favorite snacks and a little card that said "open me first" on top. Tool thought I was overdoing it. I told him to mind his business.

Saviour got dropped off from winter break with fourteen things he needed to tell me before he even got all the way through the door.

"Ma, did you know they got a rage room for kids, too? Dad took me, it was so fun, I broke like fifty things—"

"Boy, come here and give me a hug first," I said, grabbing him before he could spin off into another story.

He hugged me back hard for a second, then pulled away and looked around the living room. Tool was on the couch. Something was clearly set up: the box on the coffee table with the card on top, the little balloon bouquet Tia had helped me put together because I couldn't help myself.

Saviour squinted at all of it. "What's this?"

"Sit down," I said.

He sat down slow, suspicious, looking between me and Tool like he was trying to figure out if he was in trouble or not.

"Open the card first," I said.

He picked it up and read it out loud the way he always did, moving his lips slightly on the harder words.

Saviour, you have been the greatest adventure of my life since the day you were born. You made me a mama and I would not trade that for anything in this world. But adventures get better when you bring somebody along. Open the box.

He looked up at me. Then at Tool. Then back at me.

"Open the box, son," Tool said.

He tore into it, pulled the tissue paper out in one big handful, and held up the shirt. Read it. Read it again.

"Big Brother Loading," he said out loud.

"You're gonna be a big brother," I said, watching his face.

He looked down at the shirt again. Then back up at me. "For real?"

"For real," I said. "We're pregnant."

He nodded slow. "Okay," he said.

I waited for more. There wasn't more. He folded the shirt back up and put it in the box neat, like he was packing it away.

Tool looked at me. I looked at Tool.

"That's all you got?" I said. "Okay?"

He shrugged. "I mean, okay. That's cool, I guess."

This boy. I carried him for nine months.

***

I thought that was gonna be the end of it. We had dinner, Saviour talked about winter break, what he and Sacavè did, the rage room, watching movies, how his grandma Marlene made him clean up after himself every single morning, which he felt was excessive. Everything seemed normal.

But later that night, I was in the kitchen cleaning up when I heard Tool and Saviour talking in the living room. I slowed down and got quiet without meaning to.

"Can I ask you something, Pops?" Saviour said.

"Talk to me," Tool said.

A pause. "Can I go live with my dad?"

"Why you wanna do that?" Tool asked. His voice didn't change. Steady, calm, like the question didn't catch him off guard, even if it did.

"Because," Saviour said. Then quieter, "When the baby comes, she gonna forget about me."

My hand stopped moving on the counter.

"Who told you that?" Tool asked.

"Nobody. I just know," Saviour said. "Babies need a lot of stuff. She gonna be busy."

"Come here," Tool said. "Look at me. You hear me when I talk to you?"

"Yes, sir," Saviour said.

"Your mama ain't gon' forget about you. That ain't even possible. You was her first. You the reason she knows how to be a mama at all. You understand that?"

Saviour didn't say nothing.

"And I need you to hear me on something else," Tool said. "When I ain't here, you the man of this house. That's real. I don't give that title to everybody. I gave it to you because you earned it just by being who you are. A baby coming don't change that. If anything, it makes it more important."

"Because I'm gon' be the big brother," Saviour said, quiet.

"Because you gon' be the big brother," Tool said. "And big brothers set the example. Everything that baby gon' learn about how to move, how to treat people, how to be, they gon' learn it from watching you. That's a big deal. That ain't something you can do from your daddy's house."

The kitchen was so quiet I could hear my own heartbeat.

"You still the most important person in your mama's world," Tool said. "That don't get divided when a new baby comes. It gets bigger. You gon' have to trust me on that one."

Another pause. Then, "You promise?"

"I promise you, man," Tool said.

I stood in that kitchen and pressed my back against the counter and let my eyes water without making a sound. This man. Lord.

***

I went in there about ten minutes later like I didn't hear nothing, kissed Saviour on top of his head, and told him to go get ready for bed. He got up, hugged Tool first, then me, and went upstairs without a word.

I sat down next to Tool.

"You heard that?" he said.

"Every word," I said.

He nodded and pulled me into his side.

***

What I didn't find out until the next morning was that before Saviour went to sleep, he had texted his daddy.

dad can i come live with you

Why? What's wrong? Sacavè texted back almost immediately.

mom is having a baby and she going to forget me

I saw it when Saviour left his phone on the kitchen counter at breakfast and it lit up with Sacavè's response.

She not gon' forget you. But call me after school, we gon' talk. I love you.

I set the phone back down and didn't say a word about it.

Chapter 24

Kia

The construction crew had knocked off for the day by the time me and Tool pulled up. That was intentional. He knew I liked walking through without nobody around, no hammering, no saws going, no strangers tracking my every reaction. Just us and the bones of what was about to be our home.

I was barely showing yet, but my feet had already started giving me attitude about certain shoes, so I had on my sneakers and one of Tool's hoodies and I still felt cute about it.

We had markers. That was Tool's idea, us writing scriptures on the frames before the drywall went up. Something his mama had told him about, how you build the Word into the foundation of your home before the walls close up and you can't get back in there anymore. I thought it was the most beautiful thing I had ever heard.

We walked through the front entry and I uncapped my marker first.

The Lord will watch over your coming and going both now and forevermore. Psalm 121:8

I wrote it right there on the frame of the front door. Tool watched me do it, then did his own underneath mine.

As for me and my house, we will serve the Lord. Joshua 24:15

We moved through the house like that, stopping at each room, writing something on the frame or the stud, praying over the space before we kept moving. It felt like church in the best way.

***

Both sets of parents pulled up about thirty minutes after us. Kristen and Robert came together. My mama came with Tamia, and my uncle Mario came separate because him and Tamia were still doing that thing where they acted like being in the same car was too much to ask, but would be fine the second they got around other people.

I loved my family. I also wanted to strangle them regularly.

"Oh, this is gonna be something," my mama said, stepping through the entry and looking up at the ceiling height. "Baby, this is big."

"That's what she said," Tamia mumbled.

"Tamia," I said.

"What? I'm just standing here."

Kristen walked through with her hands clasped together, taking everything in quietly the way she did. Robert had his hands in his pockets, nodding slow like he was doing construction math in his head. Tool stayed close to his daddy, both of them moving through the space the same way: measured, analytical, seeing what wasn't there yet.

***

I took everybody on the walkthrough myself because Tool had already given me the floor, so I was gonna use it.

"Okay, so when you come in the front, you got your entryway, coat closet right here—" I pointed. "Living room opens up to the left, dining room straight ahead."

"How high are these ceilings?" Uncle Mario asked.

"Twelve feet on the main level," Tool said from somewhere behind us.

Uncle Mario nodded approvingly. That meant something coming from him.

"Kitchen is through here," I said, leading them in. "Double sink over here at the main prep area—" I pointed along the framed-out counter, "—and then a food prep sink over here on the island, too."

"Two sinks in the kitchen?" Tool said, coming up beside me with that look on his face.

"Yes," I said simply.

"So that means you gon' be cooking a lot," he said, smiling.

"Boy, if you don't—" I pointed at him. Everybody laughed.

"She got the man with two sinks," Tamia said. "That's love."

"Moving on," I said, stepping through to the next section. "Mud room off the garage, half bath down here, and then the laundry room, which is big enough to actually be in without feeling like you trapped."

My mama put her hand on her chest. "Lord. I been doing laundry in a closet for thirty years."

"You could fit a whole sitting area in here," Kristen said, looking around the laundry room. "Chair, a little table—"

"That's exactly what I want to do," I said, pointing at her. We smiled at each other.

***

We went upstairs next. I took them through the guest rooms first, two of them, each with their own bathroom.

"These are nice," Tamia said, looking around the second one. "Real nice." She looked at me. "Which one is mine?"

"You don't live here, Tamia."

"Not yet," she said, opening the closet.

"Get out the closet," I said.

Tool was already laughing.

I pulled them down the hall and stopped at the next door. "This is the quiet room," I said.

"The what?" Uncle Mario asked.

"Quiet room. No TV, no noise. Just somewhere to go when you need to think or pray or just be still for a minute," I said. "Every house needs one of those."

My mama looked at me softly. "That's beautiful, baby."

Kristen said nothing, but she put her hand on my arm for just a second as she walked past me into the room, and I felt everything in that small gesture.

***

"Saviour's room," I announced, stopping at the next door.

It was the biggest bedroom upstairs outside of the primary. His own bathroom, the window seat Tool had shown him already, closet you could practically live in.

"This boy is gon' be unbearable," Tamia said.

"He already is," Tool said.

"And this one," I said, moving to the room right next to it, "is the nursery."

The room got quiet in the way rooms do when something real settles into them. My mama started crying before I even finished the sentence.

"Mama—"

"I'm fine, I'm fine," she said, fanning her face. "I'm fine."

Tonya was not fine. But she was happy and that was all that mattered. I felt Tool come up behind me and put his hand on my stomach.

***

"Okay, and the office is down here," I said, getting back on track before I started crying too. "Big enough for two desks because we both work from home sometimes—"

"Smart," Robert said.

"And then the primary suite is at the end of the hall." I led them down. "His-and-her closets—"

"His-and-her," Uncle Mario repeated.

"Don't start," I said.

"I didn't say nothing," he said.

"His side is bigger," Tool offered.

"It is not," I said.

"Walk it off," Tool said.

I looked at him. He looked back. Robert put his hand over his mouth.

"Primary bath has a soaking tub, double vanity, separate shower, private water closet," I said, redirecting everybody. "And a sitting area by the window."

"A sitting area in the bathroom," my mama said to herself like she was memorizing it. "You deserve it, baby," she said, squeezing my hand.

***

Basement was last.

"Theater right here," Tool said, taking over when we got down the stairs. "Stadium seating, recliners—"

"How many seats?" Tamia asked.

"Twelve," Tool said.

"I'm literally moving in," Tamia said.

"Game room is through there," I said, pointing. "Bar is along this back wall—"

"Now we talking," Uncle Mario said, perking up.

"I knew that would get him," Tamia said.

"Full bar setup, mini fridge, the whole thing," Tool said, walking Uncle Mario over to the framed-out space. The two of them started talking about stools and countertop materials, and I left them to it.

***

We ended up sitting on folding chairs somebody had left in the basement, all of us just talking in the empty space, voices echoing off the unfinished walls. Tamia had found a *Bluetooth* speaker from somewhere. It turned into an unofficial gathering.

At some point, Kristen brought up Saviour's school situation. She said it casual, not pushy, but I knew it had been on her mind.

"He's doing better since winter break," I said. "But me and Sacavè have been talking about moving him to public school for third grade. Let him be around more kids that look like him."

"Nala and BJ's school is good," Tia said. She had shown up late with Nard and the kids, because of course she had. "His teacher, Ms. Darden, is amazing. She doesn't play, but she loves them kids for real."

"That fight, though," my mama said.

"I know," I said. "But that private school—" I shook my head. "It's a great education. But Saviour ain't built to be the only one in the room. He needs his people around him."

Tool nodded from across the room. "He'll be a'ight wherever he goes. But I agree with Kia on this one."

"Then it's settled," Uncle Mario said, like he had anything to do with it.

"Nothing is settled, Uncle Mario," I said.

"Sounds settled to me," he said.

Tool caught my eye across the basement and smiled. I looked around at everybody, both our families crammed into an unfinished basement, arguing and laughing and already making themselves at home in a house that wasn't even done yet.

This was exactly what I wanted. It was already more than I ever asked for.

Chapter 25

Sacavè

Britnie had referred me out two weeks after I asked her on that date. Said she had somebody good, somebody she trusted, and that she wouldn't have done it if she didn't believe it was the right move for my progress and not just for her own convenience.

I respected that about her. She didn't just say "fuck it." She was intentional about it even when it was probably the harder choice professionally.

My first session with the new therapist, Dr. Marcus Umar, older dude, salt and pepper beard, had that energy like he had heard everything and wasn't impressed by none of it, it went a'ight. Different from Britnie's style. Less warm, more direct. Like talking to a coach instead of a counselor. I wasn't mad at it.

***

I pulled up to the restaurant and checked myself in the rearview one more time. Fresh cut from earlier, all-black fit, nothing too dressy, nothing too casual. Kev-O had opinions about all of it and I had made the mistake of asking.

You going on a date with your therapist, nephew, wear something that say "I'm healed but I still got it."

I ain't even know what that meant, but somehow, I landed here and it felt right. I texted her.

Here.

She responded almost immediately.

Give me two minutes. I'm parking.

I got out and waited by the entrance. The restaurant was her pick, a spot in *Midtown* I had driven past a hundred times but never been in. Nice without being over the top. That told me something about her. She ain't need to be impressed and she ain't need to impress. She just wanted somewhere good.

I saw her coming down the sidewalk before she saw me. She was in a burgundy wrap dress, hair down, I had never seen her hair down before, always pulled back in the office, and some heels. No notepad. No professional armor. Just her.

She saw me and smiled.

"You clean up nice, Mr. Sanders," she said when she got close enough.

"You look good, Britnie," I said.

"Thank you," she said.

I opened the door and let her in first.

***

We got seated at a table near the window. Good lighting, not too loud.

The first couple minutes had that energy that first dates always had, not uncomfortable exactly, more like two people figuring out which version of themselves they were gon' be tonight now that the context had changed. In that office, I was her client and she had the structure of her profession to stand behind. Out here, it was just us and a menu and a candle between us.

"This feel weird to you?" I asked, because I wasn't gon' pretend it didn't have a little weight to it.

"A little," she said, honest. "But not bad weird."

"What kind of weird?"

"The kind where you're used to knowing somebody one way and you're curious what the other ways look like," she said, opening her menu.

"And?" I said.

She looked up. "And so far, so good."

I smiled and picked up my menu.

***

We ordered. She got the salmon. I got the ribeye, because I wasn't about to be on a date picking at something light trying to look refined. She laughed when I ordered it.

"What?" I said.

"Nothing," she said. "That's just very you."

"You know me now?"

"I've known you for almost a year, Sacavè," she said. "I know you a little bit."

"What you know about me?" I said, leaning back, giving her the floor.

She thought about it for a second. "I know you love your son more than anything in this world. I know your anger is really just fear wearing a different outfit most of the time. I know you're funnier than you let people see. And I know that when you actually let yourself be still, you're different from the person you walk around pretending to be."

The table got quiet.

"You got all that from them sessions?" I said.

"I'm observant," she said simply. "It's literally my job."

"Former job," I said. "On my case, anyway."

"Former job," she agreed, and picked up her wine glass.

***

The food came and the conversation opened up the way good conversation did when the pressure was off, easy, moving from one thing to the next without forcing it. I found out she was from *Memphis* originally, had moved to *Atlanta* for grad school and just never left. Youngest of four. Had a dog named Hendrix. Didn't watch much TV, but when she did, it was documentaries and old *Martin* episodes back-to-back with nothing in between, which I told her was the most specific combination I had ever heard in my life.

"You got kids?" I asked.

"Twin daughters. Just turned five," she said.

"They with their dad?"

Something moved across her face quick. "No. He passed," she said. Left it right there, didn't go further into it.

"I'm sorry," I said.

"It's okay," she said. "You're actually the first man I've been out with since him."

I looked at her. "First man?"

"I was with women before him," she said, just as even and unbothered as everything else she said.

I nodded slow. "So I got a lot to live up to on multiple fronts."

She laughed. "Something like that."

"What about you?" she asked. "Outside of everything I already know, what does Sacavè do when nobody's watching?"

"Music," I said.

She looked up. "Like listening, or—"

"Just listening," I said. "I'll sit in the truck for two hours if the playlist is right. Pull up somewhere quiet, cut everything off except the music."

"What kind?"

"Whatever matches where my head is at. Old R&B when I'm good. *Rod Wave* when I ain't," I said.

She smiled at that. "So I can tell exactly how you doing just by what's in your rotation."

"Pretty much," I said.

She looked at me for a second. "That was actually deep."

"I have my moments," I said.

She laughed. It was a little louder than she meant it to be and she covered her mouth after like she was surprised by it. That was the best part of the whole night right there.

***

We sat at that table for almost three hours. Didn't feel like it. The restaurant had thinned out around us and neither one of us had moved toward leaving yet.

"Can I ask you something?" I said.

"You'll ask regardless," she said.

"Why you say yes?" I said. "For real. Plenty of ways you could've shut that down in the office."

She looked at the candle for a second before she looked back at me. "Because you were the first client in a long time that felt like a real person to me instead of just a case," she said. "And I knew the moment that started happening that the professional piece was already compromised, whether either one of us acted on it or not." She paused. "So I made a choice."

"A choice to what?"

"To be honest about it instead of hiding behind my credentials," she said.

I nodded slow. "I respect that."

"I know you do," she said. "That's part of why I said yes."

***

I walked her to her car after. She stopped at her driver's side door and turned around.

"I had a good time," she said.

"Me too," I said.

"Sacavè."

"Yeah."

"Take it slow with me," she said. Not like she was scared. More like she was being honest about what she needed. "I don't do things fast."

"I got you," I said.

She looked at me like she was deciding whether she believed that. Then she nodded. I opened her car door. She got in. I closed it behind her and watched her pull off before I walked back to my truck.

Chapter 26

"Okay, looks like we got a healthy baby in there," Dr. Okafor said, moving the wand around my bump with that cold gel spread all over it like she didn't just pull it straight out the freezer.

I never got used to that part.

She printed the ultrasound and slid it into the envelope that would later tell us everything. We had decided to do an umbrella confetti photo shoot for our gender reveal. Our photographer, Milo, would be the only one to know the gender before we did. She would be the one opening the envelope the doctor gave us, so she would know what color confetti to load the umbrella with beforehand.

Overall, I was praying for a healthy baby above everything else. But I would be lying if I said I didn't already believe we were having a girl. My symptoms this time around were nothing like they were with Saviour. With him, I was all belly and emotional about absolutely everything. This time, I was all ass and thighs. I was craving *Chopped Cheese*, the smell of *Tide* detergent, and chalk. The smell of coffee made me want to throw up. And I was horny in a way that had genuinely started to concern me.

Outside of the fact that me and Tool already wanted to jump on each other at all times, pregnancy had taken it somewhere else entirely. I wanted it so bad I demanded a quickie in the bathroom during my office Christmas party. I pulled up on him on his lunch break and got some in the parking lot. Everything he did turned me on. His five percent tints kept us clear.

My growing bump made certain positions uncomfortable, but we always made it work. I rode my man like the *Kentucky Derby* and had zero apologies about it.

Tool and Saviour were both team boy. Tool wanted his first son so bad, already had the name picked out. Tevin Marcel Warren Junior. He already calls the baby "Deuce" before we even know anything. Saviour wanted a little brother because he claimed little sisters were whiny and annoying, which I found hilarious considering he got along just fine with Nala and Brielle. I didn't understand his logic, but I let him have it.

I had already decided on Teara Marie Warren just in case they didn't outnumber me.

***

"You look so handsome I could eat you up," I said to Tool as we sat in the waiting room.

We had come dressed and photo shoot ready, so my hair and makeup were already done. I just hadn't put my dress on yet because I knew Dr. Okafor needed easy access to my stomach. Tool had on his black tailored *Ralph Lauren* slacks, his black *Louis Vuitton* polo, and his all-black *Christian Louboutin* loafers. His fresh lineup with his two-strand top bun had my whole body doing things in a doctor's office that had no business happening in a doctor's office.

"You can eat me up as soon as we get home, too," Tool answered, reaching over to hold my hand while we waited.

***

As soon as we pulled up to Milo's studio parking lot, I got butterflies. I was minutes away from finding out who was in there and I could barely sit still.

Milo had the setup already done when we walked in, backdrop, lighting, all of it. She greeted us at the door with the umbrella already loaded and sealed, her face giving nothing away even though she knew everything.

"You ready?" she asked.

"I been ready," I said.

Tool helped me get into my dress in the back, a flowy cream maternity dress that hit just below the knee, bump front and center. He zipped me up slow, turned me around, and just looked at me for a second.

"You beautiful, you know that?" he said.

"You say that every time," I said.

"Because it's true every time," he said, kissing me.

Then his hands found my bump and he kissed that too, which did something to me it always did.

"Tool—"

"I know," he said, smiling against my stomach. "After."

"Promise," I said.

"On everything," he said, standing back up and kissing me one more time before Milo knocked on the door and told us she was ready.

***

"Okay, on go I need you to lift, open, and look at your wife," Milo instructed, positioning us in front of the backdrop.

"Bet," Tool agreed, taking the umbrella handle in both hands.

I stood in front of him, hands clasped together, trying to breathe normally.

"3 — 2 — 1 — go," she yelled.

When I opened my eyes, pink confetti was raining down all around us. Milo was snapping back-to-back, catching every second of it.

"Baby, it's a *girl*. I told you," I screamed.

Tool's whole face broke open. He was equal parts surprised and thrilled even without his boy. He dropped the umbrella and kissed me first, then dropped down and kissed my bump, and Milo got every single shot of it.

"Beautiful," she kept saying between clicks. "Beautiful."

He had already told me if he didn't get his boy, he would be okay, because at the rate we were going, he was going right back in for the second one.

He stood back up, pecked my lips, and said, "I'ma dump some more of my kids in your guts and make my boy."

"Ou," I said.

That man and his mouth.

"Let's wrap this up," I demanded.

Milo laughed behind her camera. "Y'all are something else," she said.

"You got your shots though, right?" I asked.

"Honey, I got everything," she said.

Chapter 27

Sacavè

"I'll take the shrimp and eggs with my eggs scrambled hard and my T-bone medium well, please," Britnie told the server.

"And for you?" She turned to me.

"Let me get the corned beef hash and a side of turkey bacon."

Me and Britnie had been dating for about four months now. I traded my in-office sessions for *FaceTime* sessions with Dr. Umar and got banned from Britnie's office entirely. Her words. She gave me a whole lecture about mixing business and pleasure before she even agreed to any of it. Said she needed to refer me out first, wouldn't budge on that, and I respected it. Once she handed me off to Dr. Umar, she made it clear we were taking things slow on her terms. I followed her lead because she was worth following. After a little bit, she finally let me all the way in, and now we were what she called "exclusively dating," which apparently was the step that came before actually being somebody's girlfriend. I ain't make the rules; I just followed them.

She was a different kind of woman than anybody I had ever been with. Cool and soft and genuine all at the same time. Floated around like everything around her was good even when it wasn't. Pure in a way that was hard to explain, not naive, just unbothered by the things that didn't deserve her energy. Everybody in my life loved her. My mama. My sister. Saviour. Even Sena, which was probably the most surprising one of all.

After Kia ambushed me with Sena on Christmas, Britnie helped us work through getting our friendship back for Saviour's sake. She knew what it felt like to have somebody disappear with no explanation, and she understood better than most what that kind of unresolved hurt could do to a kid, especially after what Saviour had expressed at the rage room. Sena was in a different headspace too by then, new baby and all. Her and Kia had gotten past their little hump. I think it eased Kia's mind more knowing Sena's baby wasn't mine. So now they kept it cordial, communicated when it was about Saviour, and left everything else alone.

Britnie only ever dated one man before me her whole life. That was Heaven and Harmonie's father. Before him, she had only ever been with women, he just charmed his way past all of that, she said. The same way I did, which she told me on our first date like it was the most natural thing in the world and then went right back to eating her food. I sat with that for a second because it meant more than she probably realized she was giving me.

He passed away. She didn't go into details about how, just that it was sudden and nothing she saw coming. She became a mental health counselor after. Made sense when you thought about it, grief had a way of pointing people toward purpose if they let it. She was still learning certain things, and I meant that in the best possible way. Everything about being with her felt new and unhurried, like she was figuring out what she liked in real time.

***

"Their service is terrible, babe," Britnie said, eyeing her empty mimosa glass.

We had been sitting at that table for a good fifteen minutes before the server even acknowledged us. Still no silverware.

Meanwhile, homegirl was running food to every surrounding table like we were invisible.

"Your fault you wanted to come here," I said. "I wanted you in that kitchen butt naked making me breakfast, and this ain't that."

She cut her eyes at me. "I told you I can't cook."

"We gotta fix that," I said.

That was another thing that had taken some adjusting. Britnie couldn't cook nothing beyond the basics of spaghetti, Alfredo, eggs if you were lucky. And I wasn't much better. Two non-cooking muhfuckas who both loved breakfast had no business being together. We had made it our thing to try different breakfast spots around the city. Some good, some mid, and some, like today, that had no business being open.

"Never again," she said, rolling her eyes toward the window.

***

The food finally came out and it looked nothing like what either one of us ordered in our heads. My corned beef hash looked like somebody had cubed up hotdogs and called it a day, nothing like what I remembered from when I was coming up. Britnie's eggs were wet and runny, which she hated more than anything, and her T-bone had clearly never seen medium well in its life.

We ate around the parts we couldn't deal with because we were hungry enough not to be too proud about it, but the vibe at that table had shifted into quiet irritation. Britnie barely complained about anything. That was one of my favorite things about her, easy to please, never made situations bigger than they needed to be. So, when she was visibly annoyed about something, you knew it was genuinely bad. This place had done the impossible.

"She better not expect a tip," Britnie said low, pushing her plate forward.

"You always leave a tip," I said.

"I used to be a server. I know the difference between a bad section and bad effort, and that—" she gestured toward the dining room, "—is bad effort."

I left a ten and called it mercy.

***

"*Mamie's Kitchen*?" I offered as we walked to the car.

"No, I'm over it," she said, taking my hand. "Just take me home."

"Your place or mine?" I asked.

She looked up at me. "Whichever one has food in the refrigerator."

"Mine," I said.

"Then yours," she said, leaning into my arm as we walked.

I unlocked the car and opened her door. She got in and I stood there for a second before closing it, looking at this woman who had somehow walked into my life through the most professionally inappropriate door possible and made everything feel lighter just by being in it.

Four months in and I still wasn't used to it.

Chapter 28

"Yes, daddy, yes." I moaned as I took good wood from my man doggy style.

This pregnancy had me wetter than I had ever been in my life, and Tool had already confirmed that the rumor about pregnant pussy being the best pussy was absolutely true. He said it with his chest, too, no hesitation.

"Gahhhdamn, woman," he said as I threw it back hard and slow.

He loved a view of my ass cheeks moving like water, and pregnancy had given me more to work with back there than I ever had. Baby girl was doing me favors. Doggy style had become my religion these days, belly comfortable, arch right, and all that extra weight distributed exactly where it needed to be.

I felt him swell up and then pull back to the tip, that slow, deliberate stroke he did when he was getting close but wasn't ready yet. Then he spread me open with both thumbs, leaned back to look at what was his, and pressed his thumb right against my asshole the way he always did when he wanted me to get there first.

"Ouuuu shiiit," I moaned into the pillow.

That man knew my body better than I did at this point.

"Cum on my dick, bae," he said low, rotating his hips in that slow circle that he knew had no defense.

I felt it building from somewhere deep, my whole body tightening around him.

"Yeah, push it out for daddy," he demanded, feeling me kegel around him.

I couldn't have stopped it if I tried.

After I got mine, he took me on a full ride to *Poundtown*, his strokes getting longer and deeper, chasing his own finish now that he had handled me first. His moans and grunts always motivated me to throw it back harder. Something about knowing I was doing that to him pushed me every single time.

"Hold on, woman, before you hurt my daughter," he said, gripping my hips to slow me down.

"This how she got here," I said, breathless, still rolling. "I put in all the work; now cum for me-e-e-e."

"*Fuck*," he yelled out, hips stuttering, hands gripping.

He dumped everything he had inside me, had been doing that since we found out I was pregnant, said there was no point in pulling out now. He held himself there for a second before pulling out slow and pressing a soft peck to my ass cheek like it deserved an apology and a thank you at the same time.

"Your freaky ass done woke my daughter up," he said, rubbing my bump gently as he felt the small flutters of movement from inside.

I laughed into the pillow. "She was already up. She stays up."

"You tired now, huh?" he asked, helping me ease down off the edge of the bed.

"As fuck," I said, still catching my breath.

***

Tool had called in late for the morning, but he couldn't miss the whole day. Without him, that warehouse would fall apart and everybody there knew it. So while he jumped in the shower, I wrapped my robe around my body and dragged myself to the kitchen to put his lunchbox together.

I thought about joining him in the shower. Then I thought about what would happen if I joined him in the shower and decided against it for the sake of his employment.

"Bae," he called out a little while later.

I was already on the couch, robe still on, dead to the world.

He came and stood over me, smelling clean and put together, while I looked like somebody had unplugged me from the wall.

"Come on, love, I ran you a bath. Go sit in there, relax, then get some rest after," he said, helping me up.

I let him walk me to the bathroom. The tub was already full, and he had put that lavender bath soak in there that he knew I loved. A towel was folded on the edge. My water bottle was sitting on the sink.

This man.

I dropped my robe and eased myself in slow, belly first, letting the warm water take all the weight I had been carrying around. I sat there with my eyes closed and my hands resting on my bump and just breathed for a few minutes. Baby girl was still moving around in there, unbothered as always.

"You good?" Tool said from the doorway.

"So good," I said, without opening my eyes.

I let that water get lukewarm before I finally climbed out, dripping and heavy. I lotioned up with a struggle, my belly getting in the way of everything, moving slow because my arms couldn't quite reach all that extra ass and thigh the way they used to. I finally crawled into those cool sheets and let out a long-ass sigh. I had exactly four hours before I had to be back at that school to pick up Saviour, and I needed every single second of that sleep to recover.

Chapter 29

The email came through at 7:43 in the morning while I was still in bed. I read it twice before I screamed.

"Baby."

He came out the bathroom with toothbrush still in his mouth, looking like something was wrong. "What happened?"

"We got our closing date," I said, holding the phone up.

He took the toothbrush out his mouth and looked at the screen. Then that smile came across his face.

"*February 14th,*" he said.

"February 14th," I repeated.

He went back to the bathroom and I heard him rinse and spit, and then he came back and got back in the bed and pulled me into him from behind.

"Our house is ready," he said into my neck.

"Our house is *ready*," I said.

Baby girl kicked right on cue, like she knew.

"Even she's excited," Tool said against my skin.

***

We called both sets of parents before we even got out of bed. Kristen screamed. My mama screamed louder. Robert said, "That's what I'm talking about," and Uncle Mario said, "It's about time," which was his way of being just as excited without showing it.

Tia texted me approximately forty-seven times in a row after Tool told her. I stopped counting after the twentieth exclamation point.

By the time we got downstairs and made breakfast, the group chat was going, and had been going, and showed no signs of stopping.

***

"We need to talk about movers," Tool said over his plate.

"I know," I said.

"I'm thinking we hire it out. Full service, they pack, they move, they unpack. We don't need to be doing all that lifting, especially with you pregnant," he said.

"I'm pregnant, not handicapped," I said.

He looked at me.

"But yes, full service is fine," I added.

"Thank you," he said. "I'll get some quotes this week. We got about six weeks between now and closing, so we got time to be strategic about it. Start sorting out what's coming, what's getting donated, what's getting thrown away."

"What's getting thrown away meaning your stuff," I said.

"Meaning whoever's stuff needs to go," he said evenly.

"Mm," I said.

He pointed at me with his fork. "I'm serious, Kia. We not moving twenty years of stuff into a brand-new house."

"Nobody got twenty years of stuff," I said.

"Your closet does," he said.

I didn't have a response for that, so I just ate my food.

***

We were still at the table when it hit me.

"Babe," I said.

"What's up?"

"What if we did the baby shower and the housewarming together?" I said.

He looked up. "Say more."

"Think about it. We gonna be moving in right around the time I'm hitting my third trimester. Both families already gonna be together, we already gonna be celebrating. Why do two separate events when we can do one big one? Housewarming so everybody can see the house, baby shower so they can celebrate Teara, all in the same day," I said.

Tool leaned back in his chair, thinking about it. "That's smart."

"I know," I said.

"You don't want your own separate shower, though?"

"I want everybody there. Both families, our friends, all of it. One big celebration," I said. "We can still do it cute, themes, decorations, registry table, the whole thing. Just combined."

"Aight," he said, nodding. "I'm with it. What's the theme?"

"I'm thinking pink and gold. Soft, elegant, not too over the top," I said.

"And the food?"

"Catered. I am not asking nobody's mama to cook for a hundred people," I said.

Tool laughed. "My mama gon' insist."

"Your mama can insist in her own kitchen on a regular Sunday," I said. "This is getting catered."

He held his hands up. "I'll let you tell her that."

"I will," I said confidently.

We both knew I was gonna let Kristen cook whatever she wanted.

***

Later that afternoon, I sat down with my planner and started mapping it out. Closing date February 14th. Move-in would realistically take a week to get fully settled. That put us at late June, early July for the combined shower and housewarming. I would be big enough to look the part, but not so far along that I would be uncomfortable.

I texted Tamia first.

We got our closing date. February 14th.

'Screaming' she texted back immediately.

I want to do a combined housewarming and baby shower. Late July.

I'm hosting she said. *Don't play with me.*

I laughed and put the phone down. Then I picked it back up and texted Tia.

Talk to your brother. We combining the housewarming and baby shower. Late July. I need you.

She called me before I could even put the phone down.

"Say less," she said when I answered. "I already got ideas."

"I know you do," I said.

"Pink and gold?"

"Pink and gold," I confirmed.

"Okay," she said again, and hung up.

Between Tamia and Tia, this thing was gonna plan itself. All I had to do was show up cute and pregnant and let everybody celebrate us. That I could do.

***

That night, after Saviour went to bed, me and Tool sat on the back porch of the house we were about to leave behind. It was warm out, sky clear, Saviour's basketball in the yard where he had left it. I had my feet in Tool's lap and my hands on my stomach and we just sat there quiet for a while, the way we did sometimes when words weren't necessary.

"You happy?" he asked after a while.

I looked at him. At this man who had walked into my life and stayed without making it complicated, who ran me baths and packed lunches and reassured my son and put his hand on my stomach like our daughter was already the most important thing in the world to him.

"I'm so happy I don't know what to do with it sometimes," I said, honest.

He squeezed my ankle. "Good," he said. "That's all I need to hear."

Baby girl kicked.

We both laughed.

Chapter 30

Sacavè

It's crazy how Britnie actually turned me into a nigga that planned dates.

I don't even know how it happened. One day I'm sitting in her office talking about my feelings, and the next I'm on the phone with Faith at midnight looking up romantic date ideas like I ain't got no street card left to protect. What this woman did to me should be studied.

It's a competition now, too, who could out-plan who. Her dates were always fun, adventurous, out-the-box type stuff. Mine had to match or top it every time, and I wasn't about to lose. I'll be honest, though: I cheated. A lot. Sena and Faith were my secret weapons. Every time I needed an idea, I was in one of their DMs like, *"Aye, what would y'all want a nigga to do for y'all?"* and they delivered every single time.

Our second date was a picnic. I paid a company to do the setup, blanket, charcuterie spread, candles, then I bought canvases and paint so we could do our own little painting after. Britnie was shocked. Said I didn't give her that energy during our sessions and that my charm scared her.

I took every bit of that credit without giving Sena or Faith a single acknowledgment. That's between me and God.

After that, the bar was set and the dates kept escalating. Dinner, Ferris wheel, horse and carriage, scooters through *Piedmont Park*, the fair. All fun, all her type of vibe. But now I wanted to do something intentional. Something that served a purpose beyond just a good time. Because if me and Britnie were gon' be anything serious long-term, spaghetti and Alfredo was not gon' cut it as a foundation. Her black card was already on thin ice the day she told me she didn't know how to make dressing or collard greens, and that she fried her chicken in a pan and then threw it in the air fryer to make sure it was cooked all the way through.

The air fryer. For chicken.

I went online and found a chef, *Chef Kool*, black man, advertised three-course soul food cooking classes in-home with the cuisine of your choice. I booked him quick, told Britnie to pull up to my spot and that I had a surprise, and said nothing else.

***

"Baby, this *Chef Kool*," I introduced as soon as she walked through the door.

She started grinning with all thirty-two, looking around at everything spread across my kitchen counter: ingredients, pots, pans, seasonings lined up like a cooking show set. For a woman who loved to eat as much as she did, the fact that she couldn't cook none of it was a personal offense to me.

"Britnie," she said, reaching her hand out to greet him, professional as always even off the clock.

She had on some fitted joggers, a cropped hoodie, and some slides. Standing about 5'4 without the heels, smooth caramel complexion, cheekbones sharp, eyes so deep and slightly slanted I was convinced some Asian ancestry was somewhere in her family tree that nobody had talked about yet. Everything about how she was put together was effortless, and it still got me every time.

I tied her apron around her waist from behind and then couldn't help myself, I gave her one good smack before putting my own apron on.

She turned around and gave me a look. *Chef Kool* shook his head like he already knew this was gon' be a long afternoon.

"Alright, so today we doing a three-course soul food spread," he said, looking back and forth between us. "And it is my understanding that neither one of y'all know how to cook."

Me and Britnie looked at each other.

"I mean, I can cook the basics to keep my daughters happy," she said, chin up. "And with that air fryer, there's really nothing I can't do."

"What's the basics?" *Chef Kool* asked.

"Spaghetti, Alfredo, sushi, homemade pizza, omelets, tacos—" she said, visibly fishing around for more items to add to the list.

Chef Kool laughed. Then he looked over at me like, *Now I understand why you called me.*

"Sushi, though," I said. "You make sushi."

"I do," she said proudly.

"But not cornbread."

"I never said that."

"Can you make cornbread?"

She paused just long enough to answer the question without saying a word.

"Alright," *Chef Kool* said, clapping his hands together. "I can't make y'all top chefs overnight, but today is a start. First course, appetizers. We doing fried catfish bites with a homemade remoulade sauce."

***

The catfish was first. *Chef Kool* walked us through the seasoning: cornmeal, garlic powder, onion powder, cayenne, salt, and pepper. Britnie stood next to me at the counter measuring everything out with the focus she usually saved for her notepad in session.

"You look like you doing math homework," I told her.

"I'm being precise," she said.

"It's cooking, not chemistry," I said.

"You said that and then burnt the first piece," *Chef Kool* said from behind us.

Britnie laughed so hard she had to put down the measuring spoon. I couldn't even be mad because he was right. I had the oil too hot and the first piece of catfish hit that pan and immediately went too dark on one side. I flipped it too fast, which *Chef Kool* said was the number-one mistake people made, moving the food before it was ready to be moved.

"Let it tell you when it's ready," he said. "Stop rushing it."

Britnie looked at me sideways.

"Don't," I said.

"I didn't say anything," she said, still smiling.

The remoulade came together better: mayo base, *Creole* mustard, hot sauce, lemon, paprika, a little horseradish. Britnie tasted it off the spoon and her eyes went wide.

"This is so good," she said. "I could put this on everything."

"That's the point," *Chef Kool* said.

We plated the catfish bites and sat down to taste before moving to the second course. Britnie picked one up, dipped it, took a bite, and closed her eyes.

"Okay," she said. "Okay, we did that."

"We?" I said. "You measured. I fried."

"Teamwork," she said.

"After I burnt the first one," I said.

"We don't talk about the first one," she said.

***

Second course was the main: smothered pork chops with rice and gravy and candied yams on the side.

The gravy was where it got serious. *Chef Kool* said gravy was the thing that separated people who could cook from people who thought they could cook. You had to build it right: butter, flour, let it get golden before you added anything liquid, then the broth slow so it didn't clump, season as you went, taste constantly.

Britnie burned the roux the first time. Flour went in too fast, butter wasn't hot enough, the whole thing clumped up in the pan. I said nothing. I just stood there.

She looked at me. "Don't."

"I didn't say a word," I said.

"Your face said it," she said.

"My face is neutral," I said.

Chef Kool reset her pan without making her feel bad about it and walked her through it again slower. Second time she got it right; the roux turned this golden brown, and when the broth hit it, the whole kitchen smelled like somebody's Sunday.

"*There* it is," *Chef Kool* said.

Britnie looked genuinely proud of herself, and something about that was the most attractive thing I had seen all day. The pork chops came out tender, yams were sweet and buttery, and we sat down for the second-course tasting, talking over each other about what we would do different and what we would keep exactly the same.

"I'm making this for my girls," Britnie said, pointing at the pork chops with her fork.

"They'll eat it?" I asked.

"Heaven will eat anything. Harmonie is picky but she loves gravy," she said.

***

Dessert was banana pudding with real vanilla wafers, homemade custard, fresh bananas, and whipped cream on top.

The custard took patience. Egg yolks, sugar, milk, vanilla, low heat, constant stirring. You couldn't walk away from it or it would scramble. Britnie stirred while I layered the wafers and bananas in the dish. We moved around each other in that kitchen like we had been doing it for years, passing things without asking, tasting off each other's spoons, Britnie humming something low under her breath while she watched that custard thicken up slow.

When it was done and chilled and we sat down to eat it, *Chef Kool* leaned back in his chair and folded his arms, satisfied.

"Y'all did good," he said. "For two people who don't cook."

"We just needed the right teacher," Britnie said.

He packed up his equipment and let himself out about twenty minutes later, leaving us at the table with the rest of the banana pudding and the house to ourselves. Britnie had her legs tucked under her in the chair, bowl in her lap, looking around the kitchen at all the pots and the mess we made.

"This was the best date I've ever been on," she said.

"Yeah?" I said.

"I learned something," she said. "I don't just have fun on your dates. I actually leave with something."

I looked at her for a second. "You taught me the same thing," I said.

She tilted her head. "In session?"

"Nah," I said. "Just in general. Being around you."

"You scary," she said softly.

"You said that on the picnic date," I said.

"Still true," she said.

I got up, took her empty bowl, and pulled her up from the chair.

"Come help me with these dishes," I said.

"Both of us?" she said.

"That's what I said."

She smiled and followed me to the sink and we stood there side by side washing pots at nine o'clock at night in my kitchen like it was the most natural thing either one of us had ever done.

Chapter 31

Sacavé

Sena named him Nyir.

Nyir James Carter, seven pounds, four ounces, born the second week of January and already running the whole household by the time I came to meet him. His daddy's last name, but Sena's whole face.

I never got to hold Saviour like this. I was locked up when he came into the world, and by the time I got to him, he was already past this stage. I had missed that with my own son and I felt the weight of it every single time I was around a newborn.

I held Nyir for the first time sitting on Sena's couch while she watched me from across the room like she was waiting to see what I was gon' do with him.

"He looks like you," I said.

"Everybody keeps saying that," she said.

"He does," I said. "He got your forehead."

"So," she said, holding her forehead.

"Ain't nothing wrong with your forehead," I said. "Stop it."

Nyir yawned and stretched his little arms out, and I felt something in my chest I wasn't prepared for, something that had been sitting unresolved in me since the day I got out and realized I had a son who had already learned to walk without me there to see it.

"You gon' be his godfather?" Sena asked, like it was a question she already knew the answer to.

"You even gotta ask?" I said.

She smiled and pulled her knees up on the couch. "I wasn't sure if you would want to. Given everything."

"Given everything, you and me still got twenty-something years between us," I said. "That don't disappear. And he ain't got nothing to do with none of that."

She nodded.

"I'm sorry again," she said. "I know I keep saying it—"

"Then stop saying it and just be good," I said. "That's all I want from you. Just be good."

She pressed her lips together and nodded. Nyir made a sound and I looked down at him; he had his eyes open now, blinking slow, staring up at me like he was trying to figure out who I was.

"What's up, nephew," I said softly.

***

Saviour met Nyir the following weekend when I brought him along for a visit. He walked in, saw the baby in the car seat, and immediately got low to look at him up close with his hands behind his back, like he already knew better than to reach out without permission.

"He so small," Saviour said.

"You were that small once," I said.

"I wasn't that small," Saviour said.

"You were smaller," I said.

He looked at me like that wasn't possible. Then he looked back at Nyir. "Can I hold him?"

"Ask *TT Sena*," I said.

He looked over his shoulder at her with those big eyes, and she melted the same way everybody melted when Saviour turned that look on them.

"Sit down on the couch first," she said.

He ran to the couch and sat down so fast I almost laughed. Sena placed Nyir in his arms and Saviour held that baby like he was made of glass, barely breathing, focused in a way that made me proud just standing there watching.

"Hi, Nyir," he said soft. "I'm your big cousin, Saviour."

I pulled my phone out and took the picture before he could tell me not to. On the drive home, Saviour was quiet, looking out the window with his hands in his lap.

"You a'ight?" I asked.

"Yeah," he said. Then after a minute, "Dad, you think my sister gonna look like that when she first come out?"

"Pretty much," I said.

He nodded slow. "I'm gon' hold her like that. Real careful."

"I know you will," I said.

He went back to the window and I kept my eyes on the road. But something about the way he said *my sister* hit me different than I expected. Maybe because I was still carrying what it felt like to hold Nyir, knowing I never got that with him. Never got to be the first person to hold my own son. Never got to be in that room. By the time I got to Saviour, he was already walking, already talking, already a whole person who had been building himself without me there to see any of it.

I started doing the math in my head, even though I knew I shouldn't have been touching that with a ten-foot pole. I looked at Kia's due date, then looked back at how far along she said she was when they dropped the news on Christmas. I traced the weeks back like a detective on a cold case until I landed right on that one night.

I thought about the heat of it. I thought about the fact that I hadn't even thought about pulling out, didn't even care to.

I tried to shove that shit back down into the dark and kept my eyes locked on the road while Saviour and I were on our way back home, but it wasn't going nowhere. It never did. Every time those numbers started adding up, the truth just sat there, quiet and heavy, coiled up in the back of my head like a snake waiting to strike.

***

I pushed it far enough back to function for the rest of the day. Fed Saviour, got him ready for bed, sat on the edge of his bed while he talked himself to sleep the way he always did, one more story, one more question, one more reason to stay up five more minutes.

After he was out, I sat in my living room in the quiet and let myself think about Britnie instead. Which was the better place for my head anyway.

She had made a comment after *Chef Kool's* class that baking was probably more my speed than cooking because it was more precise. That stuck with me. So one Saturday afternoon while Saviour was at Kia's, I pulled up a red velvet cake recipe, cleared off my counter, and decided I was gon' prove her right and use it to ask her something I had been sitting on too long.

Three hours, two ruined layers, and one near-kitchen fire later, I had something that resembled a cake if you were being generous. Lopsided. Frosting uneven. One layer halfway off the other, held together by a toothpick that was doing absolutely nothing.

But it was red velvet. From scratch.

I wrote on it with the frosting tube before she got there. Uneven letters, question mark that looked more like a comma, but it said what it needed to say:

Be my girlfriend?

I put it on the counter, straightened it as much as it was gon' straighten, and texted her to come over.

***

She walked in and looked at the cake for a minute. Then she looked at me.

"You made this," she said.

"Don't," I said.

"Sacavè—"

"I said don't."

She pressed her lips together hard, trying to hold it in. Then she laughed.

"It's leaning," she said.

"I know it's leaning," I said.

"Like, significantly leaning," she said.

"Britnie."

"Okay, okay, okay," she said, composing herself. She stepped closer and read what I wrote and her face changed completely.

I let her have it. I knew her well enough by now to know she needed to think before she spoke, and that whatever came out when she was ready was gon' be the truth.

"You got reservations," I said after a moment. "Say them."

She looked up at me. "You sure you want that?"

"I asked first. But yeah. Say what you need to say."

She took a breath. "I don't do things fast. You know that already. And I need you to understand that me saying yes to this isn't small for me. It's not the same as it would be for somebody else."

"I know that," I said.

"I need you to be patient with me on certain things," she said.

"I've been patient," I said.

"You have," she said. "And I noticed." She paused. "My girls come first. Always. Before dates, before plans, before anything. If Heaven or Harmonie need me, I go. No discussion."

"I would never ask you to do different," I said.

She nodded slow and looked back at the cake, then back at me, like she was working through the last of whatever she needed to work through.

"If this goes left—" she started.

"It won't," I said.

"You don't know that," she said.

"Nah," I said. "But I know me. And I ain't gon' do nothing to fuck up."

"You're my last heterosexual relationship," she said. "So make it count."

"I hear you," I said. "I got you."

She looked at that cake one more time, then picked up the frosting tube off the counter and wrote underneath my question in her own handwriting:

Yes.

I pulled her in and held her there.

"The cake is a nice gesture, by the way," she said into my chest.

"I know," I said.

"We're not eating it," she said.

"Already ordered food," I said.

She laughed, and this time she didn't even try to cover it.

Chapter 32

Sacavè

"You excited about your sister?" I asked Saviour on the drive over to drop him off.

He shrugged from the backseat. "I guess."

"You guess?" I said.

"I mean, yeah," he said. "I just hope she don't be too annoying."

"She gon' be a baby," I said. "Babies don't be annoying; they just be babies."

"BJ said his little sister used to cry all night and he couldn't sleep," Saviour said.

"BJ survived," I said.

Saviour didn't look convinced. He went back to his phone and I drove and let him have his reservations. He would feel different the second he held her. I already knew that.

What I didn't say out loud was that I had my own reservations about this baby that had nothing to do with crying at night.

***

Kia

Moving day had been everything I imagined and nothing I was prepared for at the same time.

The movers had done all the heavy lifting, and Tool had been everywhere at once, directing traffic, telling people where to put what, carrying boxes he had no business carrying when he was paying people to do exactly that. I had waddled around thirty-four weeks pregnant, pointing at rooms and drinking water and trying not to cry every five minutes because everything was so beautiful and so ours and so real.

By the time the sun went down and the movers were gone and Saviour was upstairs breaking in his new room like he had lived there his whole life, me and Tool stood in the middle of that kitchen and just looked at each other.

"We did it," he said.

"We did it," I said.

He pulled me in careful around my belly and held me there. I pressed my face into his chest and breathed him in and tried to stay right there in that moment and not let anything else in.

The question I had been pushing down since my first OB appointment.

I never let it stay long. I always found a reason to send it back. Me and Tool had been fucking constantly around that time, it was our honeymoon, the odds were overwhelmingly in his favor. That's what I told myself every time. And most of the time, it worked.

***

Sacavè pulled up the next afternoon to drop off some of Saviour's things he had left at his place. I met him at the door and let him in because it was the first time he was seeing the house and it would've been rude not to.

He walked in slowly, looking around, taking it all in the way people did when they were trying to absorb something bigger than they expected.

"This is nice, Kia," he said.

"Thank you," I said.

Saviour came flying down the stairs and grabbed his bag out of Sacavè's hand without breaking stride and went right back up. We both watched him go.

"You good?" Sacavè asked, turning to me.

"Tired," I said. "We just moved in yesterday."

"I know," he said. Then he looked at my belly. "How she doing?"

"Okay," I said, rubbing my side where she had been pressing her foot all morning.

He put his hand on my belly and she went crazy, flipping and turning and kicking. She barely did that for anybody else. Neither one of us said anything for a minute.

"She always do that?" he asked, his voice lower than it had been.

"Not like that," I said honestly.

He took his hand back slow. Stood there looking at the floor like he was deciding something. When he looked back up, his face had changed.

"Kia, I need to say something to you," he said.

"Sacavè—"

"Just let me say it," he said.

I pressed my lips together and waited.

"That night after your honeymoon," he said. "I didn't pull out."

The kitchen went completely still.

"I know what you gon' say," he said before I could open my mouth.

"Sacavè," I said quietly.

"I need a DNA test," he said.

I felt my throat tighten. "We can talk about—" I started.

That's when I heard it. The garage door.

We both froze. Neither one of us had heard it opening. We had been too deep into it. Tool's footsteps came through the mudroom and into the kitchen, and when he walked in and saw us both standing there, the way we were close, quiet, something unfinished hanging in the air between us, his eyes moved from me to Sacavè and back to me.

"What's good," he said, setting his keys on the counter. His voice was even, but his eyes were reading everything.

"Hey, baby," I said. Too quick. Too light.

Sacavè looked at Tool with something in his eyes that wasn't quite anger, but wasn't neutral either. "What's up," he said.

Tool nodded and walked over to me and kissed my cheek, then looked down at my belly and put his hand on it.

"How's my girl doing?" Tool asked, reaching for my belly. "Baby girl must be sleeping," he said, not feeling the movement that had been going on two minutes ago under Sacavè's hand. "She's calm."

Sacavè made a sound. Something between a laugh and a scoff. "Or she just know who her daddy really is," he mumbled.

The temperature in that kitchen dropped. I froze. Couldn't move. Couldn't speak.

Tool's hand lifted off my belly slow. He turned and looked at Sacavè with the kind of stillness that was more dangerous than noise.

"Aye, man," he said. "Watch your mouth."

Sacavè scoffed.

Chapter 33

Kia

"I'm a grown-ass man. That's some shit you say to a child," Sacavè pushed.

"Sacavè, please leave," I said, trying to diffuse the situation. But it was too late for that, and everybody in that kitchen knew it.

Tool stood off to the side, doing that thing he did with his nose when he was mad but really trying to hold his composure. Jaw tight, eyes moving between me and Sacavè like he was calculating everything in real time.

"We made love that night," Sacavè said, his eyes landing on me and staying there. "It was wrong, well, for you. Not for me. It felt right to me. Right as fuck. I need a DNA test. I need to know."

The air in that brand-new kitchen changed.

"Say bruh, this ain't about taking her from you," Sacavè continued, taking a step toward me. "I moved on. I'm happy and content. I just—"

"Sacavè," I said, barely above a whisper. The kind of whisper that said everything without saying anything.

"Nah, let him finish," Tool said, still staring at me.

"He said eno—" I started.

"When did this happen?" Tool asked. The question was directed at Sacavè, but his eyes never left my face.

Sacavè didn't answer. He was too locked into his staredown with me. The silence was loud.

"Kia," Tool's voice came out harder than I had ever heard it directed at me. The loudest he had ever spoken to me in all the time I had known him.

"Y'all handle that," Sacavè said, his voice dropping. "I want what I want. I don't need nobody raising mine." He started walking toward the front door.

"I need to sit down," I said, grabbing the countertop.

Tool wiped his hand down his face slow, then walked me over to the table by my hand and lower back. The tenderness of it against how furious he was broke something in me. He pulled the chair out and I sat down; he stood behind me, and I could feel the heat radiating off him.

***

I was so sure this mistake would go to the grave with both of us.

I was twenty-one weeks, just past the halfway mark, and I had convinced myself I was in the clear. I'd been in Sacavè's face a dozen times since Christmas, and the man hadn't breathed a word, not a look, not a hint, not even a stutter that suggested he was doing the same dirty math I was.

The only time that intrusive thought really tried to set up shop in my head was during that first OB-GYN visit. When the doctor looked at me and rattled off that estimated conception date, my heart damn near skipped a beat. I started counting back the weeks in my head, praying the numbers wouldn't lie to me.

Tool and I had been going at it like rabbits, it was our honeymoon phase, and we were making up for lost time. But the cold, hard truth I was trying to bury was that the timeline was messy. Right in that same window of time, I'd slipped up and given Sacavè that sympathy pussy. Just once. One mistake against a thousand nights with my husband, and now the calendar was starting to look like a death sentence.

One single time. A drop in the bucket compared to the endless nights I spent locked in with my husband. I had sold myself the lie that God wasn't that cruel, that He wouldn't let one lapse in judgment ruin a whole life, so I buried it deep. I didn't breathe a word to Sacavè. I kept my mouth shut with Tool. I didn't even whisper that truth to my own soul.

Teara was typically calm, movements predictable and gentle. I had even bought a *Doppler* off *Amazon* just to check her heartbeat on the nights my anxiety got the best of me. She kicked after sex like she was letting me know she felt everything, but beyond that, she stayed easy. The reaction she had to Sacavè touching my belly was something I had never felt from her before, like she was at a competition doing backflips and somersaults all at once. I felt it, and I saw Sacavè feel it, and neither one of us said what we were both thinking until he finally said it.

Everything had been so perfect. Our maternity shoot was next weekend. The shower two weeks after that. We had just moved into our dream home. Life had been everything I prayed for.

And now this.

I was even more shocked that it was Sacavè who brought it up. He had moved on. He had Britnie. He had posted them together in their chef aprons just the other day looking happy in a way I hadn't seen from him in a long time. According to Saviour, they were doing well. He seemed settled. He seemed good.

So why now?

***

"When did you cheat on me?" Tool's voice came from behind me, low and even. "And how many times?"

I heard the front door slam, the heavy thud echoing and signaling that Sacavè was finally gone. I let out a breath I didn't even know I was holding, thinking the house was empty of everyone but us.

"Tevin, calm down," I said, standing and turning toward him.

He moved fast.

His hand found my neck, the same hands that ran me baths and held my belly and opened every door, and what was usually tender was something else entirely right now. His grip tightened and I saw in his eyes something I had never seen there before. Not cruelty. Just pain wearing the face of rage.

"Is she mine," he said through his teeth, "or his?"

"I—I can't br—" I tried to get out.

"Nigga, let her go," Sacavè's voice came from the doorway. He hadn't left. He was standing there with his gun pointed, feet planted. "You thought I left so you was willing to choke her out with my son upstairs?"

"Mind your business, nigga. Get out my house," Tool said, his grip not loosening.

"St—stop," I managed.

"If she stops breathing, you gon' stop breathing too," Sacavè said. "On both my kids."

That promise made Tool's grip tighten instead of release, his eyes cutting over to Sacavè while I felt the edges of everything start to go soft.

Boom.

Tool fell back and hit the floor without a sound.

"Noooooo," I screamed, dropping down beside him, hands on his chest, his face.

The thundering of feet on the stairs hit me like a second gunshot. Fast. Desperate. My heart stopped as I realized Saviour had heard every single thing, he'd been up there the whole time, a witness to the exact moment our world fell apart.

"Sacavè, go to your son," I screamed out before he could get any further into the room.

I couldn't let him see Tool on that floor. I couldn't let him see any of this. Sacavè had frozen where he was, gun still in his hand, his face carrying the look of a man who had already felt the weight of what he just did before the sound even finished echoing through our brand-new home. He backed toward the stairs slowly.

"Saviour," he said when he met him at the bottom. His voice was different. Controlled. The voice he saved for his son. "Call 911. Tell them you heard a gunshot and your mama screamed. Can you do that for me?"

Saviour stared back at him with tears already falling, eyes darting past him toward the kitchen.

"Your mother is okay, son. I promise. Go call," Sacavè said.

I heard Saviour's feet on the stairs again, going back up. I still had my hands on Tool. Still felt a pulse, faint but there. His chest was moving but his eyes weren't open and he wasn't responding, and I knew every second mattered.

"I'm so sorry," I said against his face. "Tool, stay with me. Please. Please stay with me."

I pressed my forehead to his and held on.

"She's yours," I whispered. "She's yours, I promise she's yours. She needs you. We need you. Please stay with us."

<table>
<tr><td>$699
Editing
Cover Design
Formatting</td><td>$1000
Typing
Editing
Cover Design
Formatting
Upload eBooks to Amazon
Upload Paperback to Amazon</td></tr>
<tr><td>ADVANCE PACKAGE
$1,400
Typing
Editing (line editing/content)
Cover Design
Formatting
Copyright Registration
Proofreading
Upload eBooks to Amazon
Upload Paperback to Amazon</td><td>LDP SUPREME PACKAGE
$1,700
Typing
Editing (line editing/content)
Cover Design
Formatting
Copyright Registration
Proofreading
Set up Amazon Account
Upload eBooks to Amazon
Upload Paperback to Amazon
Advertise on LDP's Amazon and Facebook Page</td></tr>
</table>

***

Other services available upon request.
Additional charges may apply

Lock Down Publications
P.O. Box 944
Stockbridge, GA 30281-9998
Phone: 470 303-9761
Email: lockdownpublications@gmail.com

Submission Guideline

Submit the first three chapters of your completed manuscript to ldpsubmissions@gmail.com. In the subject line add **Your Book's Title**. The manuscript must be in a Word Doc file and sent as an attachment. Document should be in Times New Roman, double spaced, and in size 12 font. Also, provide your synopsis and full contact information. If sending multiple submissions, they must each be in a separate email.

Have a story but no way to send it electronically? You can still submit to LDP/Ca$h Presents. Send in the first three chapters, written or typed, of your completed manuscript to:

LDP: Submissions Dept
P.O. Box 944
Stockbridge, GA 30281-9998

DO NOT send original manuscript. Must be a duplicate. Provide your synopsis and a cover letter containing your full contact information.

Thanks for considering LDP and Ca$h Presents.

NEW RELEASES

BLOODLINE OF A SAVAGE 1-3
THESE VICIOUS STREETS 1-3
RELENTLESS GOON 1-3
SOULLESS GOON 1&2
BY PRINCE A. TAUHID

THE BUTTERFLY MAFIA 3
BY FUMIYA PAYNE

A THUG'S STREET PRINCESS 1&2
BY MEESHA

CITY OF SMOKE 1-3
BY MOLOTTI

GET IT IN SLUGS 1 &2
BY B. STALL

STANDING ON HER BUSINESS 1&2
BY DG SANTANA

STEPPERS 1,2&3
THE REAL BADDIES OF CHI-RAQ 1-3
BY KING RIO

THE LANE 1-3
BY KEN-KEN SPENCE

THUG OF SPADES 1&2
LOVE IN THE TRENCHES 1&2
CORNER BOYS 1&2
ONCE YOU GO GANGSTA
PROTÉGÉ OF A LEGEND 1- 3
BY COREY ROBINSON

TIL DEATH 3
BY ARYANNA

THE BIRTH OF A GANGSTER 4
BY DELMONT PLAYER

PRODUCT OF THE STREETS 1-3
BY DEMOND "MONEY" ANDERSON

MONEY HUNGRY DEMONS 1-2
BY TRANAY ADAMS

TRAP STARS
BY B. SHELLY

HUB CITY MENACE 1-4
BY J. WHITE

A THUGGISH PASSION 1&2
LAND OF DA HOOLIGANZ 1-4
KILLAZ ON STANDBY 1&2
FRESH OFF DA PORCH 1-3
SECURE DA BAG
AMBITIONS OF A SLIDER
FOR MY ENEMIES SAKE
SOULLESS GOON 1&2
FO'EVA ROLLIN 1-4
BY ASSA RAYMOND BAKER

THE LEVEL UP 1&2
BY LUXURY KING

HUNGRY FOR MONEY 1&2
SLIMBOS

QUEEN OF NAPTOWN 1&2
THA TAKEOVER 1-3
BY KEITH CHANDLER

DRILL CITY 1&2
BY ZAY'TOWVEN

LOVE ME OR LET ME GO
BY R. FACEY

SAVAGE DREAMZ
BY KING DAVID

MONEY AND DEAD HOMIES
BY DERRICK SUMMERS

WHITE BOYS
BY BANDEMIC

A THUGS STREET PRINCESS 3 Coming Soon
BY MEESHA

BETRAYAL OF A G 2
BY RAY VINCI

SAVAGE FAMILY EMPIRE 1&2
SOULLESS GOON 1&2
THE DIRTY SIDE OF MONEY 1,2&3
BY PRINCE

BY THE TRUCKLOAD 1-4 COMING SOON
T SOULLESS GOON 1&2
IPPIN' THE SCALES 1-4
BAD BITCHES WIT GUNZ 1-3
PROBLEM SOLVED 1-3
THE GIRLRILLA AND HER N*GGA
THE SINGLE LADIES
BY CHRISTOPHER "DIESEL" HORNEZES

AVAILABLE NOW

RESTRAINING ORDER 1 & 2
BY CA$H & COFFEE

LOVE KNOWS NO BOUNDARIES 1-3
BY COFFEE

RAISED AS A GOON I, II, III & IV
BRED BY THE SLUMS I, II, III
BLAST FOR ME I & II
ROTTEN TO THE CORE I II III
A BRONX TALE I, II, III
DUFFLE BAG CARTEL I II III IV V VI
HEARTLESS GOON I II III IV V
A SAVAGE DOPEBOY I II
DRUG LORDS I II III
CUTTHROAT MAFIA I II
KING OF THE TRENCHES
BY GHOST

LAY IT DOWN I & II
LAST OF A DYING BREED I II
BLOOD STAINS OF A SHOTTA I & II III
BY JAMAICA

LOYAL TO THE GAME I II III
LIFE OF SIN I, II III
BY TJ & JELISSA

IF LOVING HIM IS WRONG…I & II
LOVE ME EVEN WHEN IT HURTS I II III
BY JELISSA

PUSH IT TO THE LIMIT
BY BRE' HAYES

BLOODY COMMAS I & II
SKI MASK CARTEL I, II & III
KING OF NEW YORK I II, III IV V
RISE TO POWER I II III
COKE KINGS I II III IV V
BORN HEARTLESS I II III IV
KING OF THE TRAP I II
BY T.J. EDWARDS

WHEN THE STREETS CLAP BACK I & II III
THE HEART OF A SAVAGE I II III IV
MONEY MAFIA I II
LOYAL TO THE SOIL I II III
BY JIBRIL WILLIAMS

A DISTINGUISHED THUG STOLE MY HEART I II & III
LOVE SHOULDN'T HURT I II III IV
RENEGADE BOYS 1-4
PAID IN KARMA 1-3
SAVAGE STORMS 1-3
AN UNFORESEEN LOVE 1-3
BABY, I'M WINTERTIME COLD 1-3
A THUG'S STREET PRINCESS 1,2&3
EMBRACING THE LOVE OF A BOSS
BY MEESHA

A GANGSTER'S CODE 1-3
A GANGSTER'S SYN 1-3
THE SAVAGE LIFE 1-3
CHAINED TO THE STREETS 1-3
BLOOD ON THE MONEY 1-3
A GANGSTA'S PAIN 1-3
BEAUTIFUL LIES AND UGLY TRUTHS
CHURCH IN THESE STREETS
BY J-BLUNT

CUM FOR ME 1-8
AN LDP EROTICA COLLABORATION

BLOOD OF A BOSS 1-5
SHADOWS OF THE GAME
TRAP BASTARD
BY ASKARI

THE STREETS BLEED MURDER 1-3
THE HEART OF A GANGSTA 1-3
BY JERRY JACKSON

WHEN A GOOD GIRL GOES BAD
BY ADRIENNE

THE COST OF LOYALTY 1-3
BY KWELI

BRIDE OF A HUSTLA 1-3
THE FETTI GIRLS 1-3
CORRUPTED BY A GANGSTA 1-4
BLINDED BY HIS LOVE
THE PRICE YOU PAY FOR LOVE 1-3
DOPE GIRL MAGIC 1-3
BY DESTINY SKAI

A KINGPIN'S AMBITION
A KINGPIN'S AMBITION II
I MURDER FOR THE DOUGH
BY AMBITIOUS

TRUE SAVAGE 1-7
DOPE BOY MAGIC 1-3
MIDNIGHT CARTEL 1-3
CITY OF KINGZ 1&2
NIGHTMARE ON SILENT AVE
THE PLUG OF LIL MEXICO 1&2
CLASSIC CITY
BY CHRIS GREEN

GANGSTA CITY
BY TEDDY DUKE

BACK IN BLOOD
SEX, MURDER AND GOD 1&2
COUNTDOWN OF A KILLA 1&2
GUNS DOWN, BOTTOMS UP 1&2
BY LO-LIFE

A GANGSTER'S REVENGE 1-4
THE BOSS MAN'S DAUGHTERS 1-5
A SAVAGE LOVE 1&2
BAE BELONGS TO ME 1&2
A HUSTLER'S DECEIT 1-3
WHAT BAD BITCHES DO 1-3
SOUL OF A MONSTER 1-3
KILL ZONE
A DOPE BOY'S QUEEN 1-3
TIL DEATH 1-3
IMMA DIE BOUT MINE 1-6
DYING FOR LIKES 1&2
KILLA CREW 1&2
BY ARYANNA

A DOPEBOY'S PRAYER
BY EDDIE "WOLF" LEE

THE KING CARTEL 1-3
BY FRANK GRESHAM

THESE NIGGAS AIN'T LOYAL 1-3
BY NIKKI TEE

GANGSTA SHYT 1-3
BY CATO

THE ULTIMATE BETRAYAL
BY PHOENIX

BOSS'N UP 1-3
BY ROYAL NICOLE

I LOVE YOU TO DEATH
BY DESTINY J

I RIDE FOR MY HITTA
I STILL RIDE FOR MY HITTA
BY MISTY HOLT

LOVE & CHASIN' PAPER
BY QAY CROCKETT

TO DIE IN VAIN
SINS OF A HUSTLA
BY ASAD

BROOKLYN HUSTLAZ
BY BOOGSY MORINA

A DRUG KING AND HIS DIAMOND 1-3
A DOPEMAN'S RICHES
HER MAN, MINE'S TOO 1&2
CASH MONEY HO'S
THE WIFEY I USED TO BE 1&2
PRETTY GIRLS DO NASTY THINGS
BY NICOLE GOOSBY

LIPSTICK KILLAH 1-3
CRIME OF PASSION 1-3
FRIEND OR FOE 1-3
BY MIMI

TRAPHOUSE KING 1-3
KINGPIN KILLAZ 1-3
STREET KINGS 1&2
PAID IN BLOOD 1&2
CARTEL KILLAZ 1-3
DOPE GODS 1&2
BY HOOD RICH

BROOKLYN ON LOCK 1 & 2
BY SONOVIA

THE STREETS ARE CALLING
BY DUQUIE WILSON

STEADY MOBBN' 1-3
THE STREETS STAINED MY SOUL 1-3
BY MARCELLUS ALLEN

WHO SHOT YA 1-3
SON OF A DOPE FIEND 1-4
HEAVEN GOT A GHETTO 1&2
SKI MASK MONEY 1&2
BY RENTA

GORILLAZ IN THE BAY 1-4
TEARS OF A GANGSTA 1/&2
3X KRAZY 1&2
STRAIGHT BEAST MODE 1&2
BY DE'KARI

SLAUGHTER GANG 1-3
RUTHLESS HEART 1-3
BY WILLIE SLAUGHTER

GOD BLESS THE TRAPPERS 1-3
THESE SCANDALOUS STREETS 1-3
FEAR MY GANGSTA 1-5
THESE STREETS DON'T LOVE NOBODY 1-2
BURY ME A G 1-5
A GANGSTA'S EMPIRE 1-4
THE DOPEMAN'S BODYGAURD 1&2
THE REALEST KILLAZ 1-3
THE LAST OF THE OGS 1-3
BY TRANAY ADAMS

MARRIED TO A BOSS 1-3
BY DESTINY SKAI & CHRIS GREEN

TRIGGADALE 1-3
MURDA WAS THE CASE 1-3
BY ELIJAH R. FREEMAN

KINGZ OF THE GAME 1-7
CRIME BOSS 1-4
BY PLAYA RAY

FUK SHYT
BY BLAKK DIAMOND

DON'T F#CK WITH MY HEART 1&2
BY LINNEA

ADDICTED TO THE DRAMA 1-3
IN THE ARM OF HIS BOSS
BY JAMILA

YAYO 1-4
A SHOOTER'S AMBITION 1&2
BRED IN THE GAME
BY S. ALLEN

TRAP GOD 1-3
RICH $AVAGE 1-3
MONEY IN THE GRAVE 1-3
CARTEL MONEY 1&2
BY MARTELL TROUBLESOME BOLDEN

FOREVER GANGSTA 1&2
GLOCKS ON SATIN SHEETS 1&2
BY ADRIAN DULAN

TOE TAGZ 1-4
LEVELS TO THIS SHYT 1&2
IT'S JUST ME AND YOU
BY AH'MILLION

LOYALTY AIN'T PROMISED 1&2
BY KEITH WILLIAMS

KINGPIN DREAMS 1-3
RAN OFF ON DA PLUG
BY PAPER BOI RARI

THE STREETS MADE ME 1-3
BY LARRY D. WRIGHT

CONFESSIONS OF A GANGSTA 1-4
CONFESSIONS OF A JACKBOY 1-3
CONFESSIONS OF A HITMAN
CONFESSIONS OF A DOPE BOY
BY NICHOLAS LOCK

I'M NOTHING WITHOUT HIS LOVE
SINS OF A THUG
TO THE THUG I LOVED BEFORE
A GANGSTA SAVED XMAS
IN A HUSTLER I TRUST
BY MONET DRAGUN

QUIET MONEY 1-3
THUG LIFE 1-3
EXTENDED CLIP 1&2
A GANGSTA'S PARADISE
BY TRAI'QUAN

CAUGHT UP IN THE LIFE 1-3
THE STREETS NEVER LET GO 1-3
BY ROBERT BAPTISTE

NEW TO THE GAME 1-3
MONEY, MURDER & MEMORIES 1-3
BY MALIK D. RICE

CREAM 2-3
THE STREETS WILL TALK
BY YOLANDA MOORE

THE STREETS WILL NEVER CLOSE 1-3
BY K'AJJI

LIFE OF A SAVAGE 1-4
A GANGSTA'S QUR'AN 1-4
MURDA SEASON 1-3
GANGLAND CARTEL 1-3
CHI'RAQ GANGSTAS 1-4
KILLERS ON ELM STREET 1-3
JACK BOYZ N DA BRONX 1-3
A DOPEBOY'S DREAM 1-3
JACK BOYS VS DOPE BOYS 1-3
COKE GIRLZ
COKE BOYS
SOSA GANG 1&2
BRONX SAVAGES
BODYMORE KINGPINS
BLOOD OF A GOON
BY ROMELL TUKES

CONCRETE KILLA 1-3
VICIOUS LOYALTY 1-3
BLOODY MONEY BAGS
BY KINGPEN

THE ULTIMATE SACRIFICE 1-6
KHADIFI
IF YOU CROSS ME ONCE 1-3
ANGEL 1-4
IN THE BLINK OF AN EYE
BY ANTHONY FIELDS

THE LIFE OF A HOOD STAR
BY CA$H & RASHIA WILSON

NIGHTMARES OF A HUSTLA 1-3
BLOOD AND GAMES 1&2
BY KING DREAM

HARD AND RUTHLESS 1&2
MOB TOWN 251
THE BILLIONAIRE BENTLEYS 1-3
REAL G'S MOVE IN SILENCE
BY VON DIESEL

MOB TIES 1-7
SOUL OF A HUSTLER, HEART OF A KILLER 1-3
GORILLAZ IN THE TRENCHES
OOPS CRY TOO 1-3
THE DAUGHTER OF A CARTEL BOSS 1&2
BY SAYNOMORE

BODYMORE MURDERLAND 1-3
THE BIRTH OF A GANGSTER 1-4
BY DELMONT PLAYER

FOR THE LOVE OF A BOSS 1&2
BY C. D. BLUE

KILLA KOUNTY 1-5
TENDER 1&2
BY KHUFU

MOBBED UP 1-4
THE BRICK MAN 1-5
THE COCAINE PRINCESS 1-10
STEPPERS 1-3
SUPER GREMLIN 1-5
A GANGSTA'S SON
THE CONNECT'S SECRET
BY KING RIO

MONEY GAME 1&2
BY SMOOVE DOLLA

A GANGSTA'S KARMA 1-5
BY FLAME

KING OF THE TRENCHES 1-3
By GHOST & TRANAY ADAMS

QUEEN OF THE ZOO 1&2
BY BLACK MIGO

GRIMEY WAYS 1-3
BETRAYAL OF A G
BY RAY VINCI

XMAS WITH AN ATL SHOOTER
BY CA$H & DESTINY SKAI

KING KILLA 1&2
PAPER, ROCK, SNAKES
BY VINCENT "VITTO" HOLLOWAY

BETRAYAL OF A THUG 1&2
BY FRE$H

COUNTDOWN OF A KILLA 1&2
SEX, MURDER AND GOD 1&2
GUNS DOWN, BOTTOMS UP 1&2
BY LO-LIFE

FOR THE LOVE OF BLOOD 1-4
BY JAMEL MITCHELL

HOOD CONSIGLIERE 1-3
NO TIME FOR ERROR 1&2
REAL
BY KEESE

THE PLUG'S RUTHLESS DAUGHTER 1,2&3
REDEMPTION IN THE STREETS
BY TONY DANIELS

BORN IN THE GRAVE 1-3
CRIME PAYS 1-3
BY SELF MADE TAY

MOAN IN MY MOUTH
BY XTASY

TORN BETWEEN A GANGSTER AND A GENTLEMAN
BY J-BLUNT

LOYALTY IS EVERYTHING 1-3
CITY OF SMOKE 1-3
BY MOLOTTI

HERE TODAY GONE TOMORROW 1&2
BY FLY ROCK

WOMEN LIE MEN LIE 1-4
FIFTY SHADES OF SNOW 1-3
STACK BEFORE YOU SPLURGE
GIRLS FALL LIKE DOMINOES
NAÏVE TO THE STREETS
BY ROY MILLIGAN

PILLOW PRINCESS
BY S. HAWKINS

THE BUTTERFLY MAFIA 1-3
SALUTE MY SAVAGERY 1&2
BY FUMIYA PAYNE

THE LANE 1&2
BY KEN-KEN SPENCE

THE PUSSY TRAP 1-5
BY NENE CAPRI

DIRTY DNA
BY BLAQUE

SANCTIFIED AND HORNY
BY XTASY

BOOKS BY LDP'S CEO, CA$H

TRUST IN NO MAN
TRUST IN NO MAN 2
TRUST IN NO MAN 3
BONDED BY BLOOD
SHORTY GOT A THUG
THUGS CRY
THUGS CRY 2
THUGS CRY 3
TRUST NO BITCH
TRUST NO BITCH 2
TRUST NO BITCH 3
TIL MY CASKET DROPS
RESTRAINING ORDER
RESTRAINING ORDER 2
IN LOVE WITH A CONVICT
LIFE OF A HOOD STAR
XMAS WITH AN ATL SHOOTER

www.ingramcontent.com/pod-product-compliance
Lightning Source LLC
LaVergne TN
LVHW020710110826
845149LV00012B/2190
* 9 7 8 1 9 7 1 7 7 0 2 5 3 *